Delta Daniels—diet guru and author of seven previously published diet books—popped another chocolate-cream candy into her mouth. She continued typing furiously, her jaws working rhythmically with the click of the word-processor keys. As she built to a rousing, inspirational finish, she stuffed another chocolate into her mouth.

Delta sat back, exhausted. It was done. Life was good. Smiling, she closed her eyes and took a satisfied breath, rubbing the kinks out of her neck and absently reaching for another Carnaby Chocolate Cream. She patted each row in the candy box, fingered each little paper cup, then reluctantly opened her eyes. They were all gone.

She patted her midriff, then frowned. Slowly she looked down at herself. There she was, one of the most successful diet counselors in the country, fat as a pregnant toad.

Dear Reader:

Welcome! You hold in your hand a Silhouette Desire—your ticket to a whole new world of reading pleasure.

A Silhouette Desire is a sensuous, contemporary romance about passions, problems and the ultimate power of love. It is about today's woman—intelligent, successful, giving—but it is also the story of a romance between two people who are strong enough to follow their own individual paths, yet strong enough to compromise, as well.

These books are written by, for and about every woman that you are—wife, mother, sister, lover, daughter, career woman. A Silhouette Desire heroine must face the same challenges, achieve the same successes, in her story as you do in your own life.

The Silhouette reader is not afraid to enjoy herself. She knows when to take things seriously and when to indulge in a fantasy world. With six books a month, Silhouette Desire strives to meet her many moods, but each book is always a compelling love story.

Make a commitment to romance—go wild with Silhouette Desire!

Best ,

Isabel Swift
Senior Editor & Editorial Coordinator

KATHERINE GRANGER
He Loves Me,
He Loves Me Not

Silhouette Desire

Published by Silhouette Books New York

America's Publisher of Contemporary Romance

SILHOUETTE BOOKS
300 East 42nd St., New York, N.Y. 10017

ISBN: 0-373-05428-9

First Silhouette Books printing June 1988

KATHERINE GRANGER

had never read a romance until 1975, when a friend dumped a grocery bag filled with them in her living room and suggested she might enjoy them. Hooked with the very first one, Ms. Granger became a closet romance writer three years later. When she isn't writing, she teaches creative writing and composition at a community college and freshman composition at her alma mater. Katherine lives in Connecticut with her cat, Barnaby. She enjoys movies, theater, golf, the Boston Red Sox, weekends at New England country inns and visits to Cape Cod.

One

On the next-to-last page of her latest diet book, Delta Daniels—diet guru and author of seven previously published diet books—popped another chocolate cream candy into her mouth. She continued typing furiously, her jaws working rhythmically with the click of the word processor keys.

As she built to a rousing, inspirational finish, she stuffed another chocolate into her mouth, chewing frantically, basking in her chocolate-induced euphoria. Heading into the final paragraph, she spoke the words out loud from around the comforting ooze of the extra thick, extra chocolaty Carnaby Chocolate Cream: "Remember, *you* are in control of your destiny! You, too, can be slim, svelte, sexually appealing. You, too, can know the satisfaction of admiring glances, can become the envy of your friends. Don't live to eat, eat to live—beautifully, happily, and best of all, slenderly, in nothing more than a size eight or ten...."

Delta sat back, exhausted. It was done, finished, her eighth opus, the latest in a long string of increasingly successful books. Life was good. Smiling, she closed her green eyes and took a satisfied breath, rubbing the kinks out of her neck and absently reaching for another Carnaby Chocolate Cream. She patted each row in the candy box, fingered each little paper cup, then reluctantly opened her eyes. Damn. They were all gone.

She patted her midriff, then frowned. Slowly she looked down at herself, then sighed. She wore an aqua sweatshirt and sweatpants, but the elastic waistband was straining at the seams. Above the waistband, her midriff was a swelling bulge, only slightly smaller than the curve of her breasts. She looked like a sausage tightly packed in its casing, or a Thanksgiving turkey, trussed and waiting for the oven.

When had it happened? Sometime during the past ten weeks, while working on her latest diet book, she'd succumbed to the battle of the bulge, and as usual, she'd lost. There was no escaping it—she was fat. Oh, maybe not obese, but she sure wasn't slim and svelte, wasn't the sexually appealing woman she'd just exhorted her readers to become.

She turned to look in the full-length mirror opposite her desk. Yup. There she was, one of the most successful diet counselors in the country, fat as a pregnant toad. She arched a wry brow and examined herself sardonically, noting her flawless complexion and curly brown hair, tousled now and framing her oval face. She noted the lush curve of her perfectly formed mouth, and her retroussé nose, but they didn't make her feel any better. Her face wasn't the problem; it never had been. It was her body: instead of being firm and flat, it was soft and flabby. When it came right down to it, she was an excellent replica of the Pillsbury doughboy. Poke her in the ribs and your finger could be lost for days....

The phone rang and she reached for it thankfully. Anything would be better than facing herself.

"Delta? Marcia Howard. Have you finished your book yet?"

Marcia was Delta's editor at Phoenix Books. "Just typed the last paragraph, not five minutes ago," Delta answered, propping her elbow on her desk and nestling her chin in her hand.

"Wonderful! But hold on to your hat, Delta. The best news is yet to come."

"Mmm?" Delta picked a crumb from the Carnaby Chocolate Cream box and licked it off her finger. "What's happening?"

"Did you see the *New York Times Book Review* Sunday?"

"Marcia, be real. When I write, I hibernate, you know that. We could have declared war. The stock market could have crashed and I wouldn't have known about it."

"Guess whose book is number one on the nonfiction list?" Marcia asked coyly.

"Jane Fonda's," she said, then shook her head. "No, wait. Who's that movie star who's got the latest exercise book out?"

"Movie star, hell," Marcia Howard said. "It's you, you ninny! *The Last Diet Book You'll Ever Need* by Delta Daniels."

"You're kidding."

"Oh, no, I'm not, honey. Your ship's come in. All that hard work's finally paid off. You're number one, kid, and you know what that means, don't you?"

"More money?" Delta asked hopefully.

"Money is the least of it. I'm talkin' nationwide TV, the entire talk show circuit—*The Mary Vale Show*, *Ted Sullivan's...*" She lowered her voice to a reverent level: *"Mornings with Morton."*

"Mornings with Morton*?"* Delta swallowed. Bill Morton was the writer's dream come true. You went on Morton's show with three thousand books sold, and a month later you'd sold a half a million. The women who watched Morton loved him, loved his mop of blond hair, his pipe, his tweed jackets, the earnest look in his brown eyes, the endearing cowlick. They loved him, and therefore loved his guests. And when they loved his guests, they bought his

guests' books. And that meant money. Big bucks. Capital *B*.

"I can't go on national television, Marcia," Delta said, her eyes widening as she stared at herself in the full-length mirror. She was never far from a mirror. She attracted the damn things like magnets. It was like an ancient curse.

"What do you mean you can't?" Marcia said, chortling. "You're goin', honey. Three weeks from today. It's all set."

Delta groaned and wilted in her chair. "Marcia, you don't understand. I've . . . um . . ."

"Oh, God," Marcia said. "You've been eating again."

"Well, you don't have to say it like that!" Delta said, sitting up. "You'd think I'd been drinking!"

"With you, Delta, food is alcohol." Marcia sighed gustily. "Well, there's nothing to be done about it now. You'll have to go on one of your diets and not eat a damn thing for the next three weeks. Is that clear? Nothing. No pastry, Delta. No pudding. None of those damned Carnaby Chocolate Creams."

Delta eyed the empty candy box and winced. Going without Carnaby's chocolate was like cutting off her air supply. Then she squared her shoulders and sat up. What the hell! She'd done it before. Like millions of other women, she'd lost the weight she needed to lose dozens of times, and she could do it again. Then she slumped back in the chair. Who was she kidding? In the past she'd gone into hiding for three months and taken off the pounds. How could she ever expect to lose all that weight in three weeks?

"I can't do it, Marcia," Delta said. "It's impossible. I look like a blimp. If Goodyear stumbled onto me, they'd swear I was theirs."

"Darn you, Delta Daniels," Marcia said. "You listen to me. You're going to lose it, and I don't care if I personally have to come out there and sew your mouth shut. We're talkin' big time, here, Delta, not some two-bit local cable channel. Morton is *it*, and we're not gonna blow it when we're this close. You lose that weight, Delta, or you'll never see the light of another publishing house as long as you live, understand? This latest book you just finished? Kiss it goodbye. It's back to clerking, typing, or whatever you did before you hit the big time. Is that sufficiently clear?''

Delta nodded, eyebrows raised. "Yeah, that's pretty clear, Marcia.''

"Good. Now do it. I'll call you one week from today. If you haven't lost one-third of that weight you've gained, you're dead meat.'' With that, Marcia Howard slammed the receiver down, leaving Delta holding the phone, her ear ringing.

Sighing, Delta hung up, then sat massaging her ear. Well, here she was, back at square one, only this time the challenge to lose weight was even more important than usual. Her future depended on it. Her livelihood was threatened.

Delta looked around the pine-paneled study, taking in the cheerful chintz-covered furniture, the fieldstone fireplace where a fire crackled on the hearth, the sliding glass doors that opened onto a deck overlooking the sweeping private beach on Cape Cod's north shore. She'd bought this place with the money she'd received from her diet books, but now her credibility was on the line. A diet guru couldn't be fat; it wasn't cricket. All her faithful customers, everyone who bought her books and believed in her, would be extremely irritated.

She looked back at the word processor where the final page of *The Delta Diet*—subtitled *Lose Weight the Delta Daniels Way*—seemed to reproach her. She was a fraud, no better than a dime-store grifter running a street scam. She'd made a million dollars telling people how to lose weight, but she herself was fat.

She looked in the mirror. Perhaps she wasn't obese, but another box or two of Carnaby Chocolate Creams could throw her over the delicate line she trod so uneasily. Groaning, she stuck her tongue out at herself and slid lower in the chair, taking perverse delight in seeing her stomach protrude, like a great white whale surfacing.

She groaned again and sat up. Chiding herself wasn't getting her anywhere. She had to *do* something. But what?

She couldn't very well join the local health club. She'd be laughed out of the place when it was discovered that she was *the* Delta Daniels. What a coup for the Better Bodee Health Club chain, to be able to claim they'd shaped up Delta Daniels. No, she needed something more private, anonymous, like a personal trainer.

She screwed up her mouth thoughtfully. Hmm. That's how all the Hollywood stars did it. They hired someone to come in every day and shape them up, someone who oversaw their every move, made them drink carrot juice and eat those dreadful rice cakes. Delta shuddered at the thought. Once, in a fit of guilt and good intentions, she'd bought some of those rice cakes, but when she'd bitten into one, she'd sworn she was gnawing on Styrofoam.

She reached for the phone book and flipped to the yellow pages, then ran her finger down the health club column until she came to "Kyle Frederick, Personal Fitness Trainer." Eureka! She dialed with trembling fingers. The phone was answered on the first ring in a straightforward, no-nonsense style: "Frederick."

Delta arched a brow. The voice was deep, the tone almost curt. She pictured a Marine drill sergeant and didn't know whether to cheer or cry. "Mr. Frederick, my name is Delta Daniels, and I need help."

There was a low chuckle, then, "What kind of help, Mrs. Daniels? How bad's the damage?"

"The damage?" She was momentarily distracted by being called Mrs. Daniels. It was a married world, and at thirty-two she was still single; she just didn't fit in.

"How much weight do you have to lose?" Kyle Frederick's question called her back from her thoughts.

"Oh." She wriggled comfortably in her seat. When she talked about her weight, she was on solid ground. "I'd say twenty pounds would do it."

"Why don't I make an appointment for you to come in to my gym sometime next week and we can talk about a fitness regime and—"

"Next week? Oh, no, Mr. Frederick, this is a lot more serious than that. I've got to see you soon. Right now. Today."

Silence greeted her statement. To her, it seemed a disapproving silence. Kyle Frederick was probably one of those muscle-bound men with a brain the size of a pea. He probably measured good looks in a woman by the ratio of bust to waist size. Something about his name was familiar. Delta wrinkled her brow, trying to remember where she'd heard it. Maybe she'd read an article in the local paper about him. She decided to start over. "You see, Mr. Frederick, this is kind of a special case."

"Mrs. Daniels," he said tiredly, "*every* case is kind of special."

She faltered, then forced a bright tone. "Well, yes, I'm sure. No one would know better than I, but you see, this truly *is* special. I'm Delta Daniels. *The* Delta Daniels." More silence. She sat back and frowned.

"Is the name supposed to mean something, Mrs. Daniels?" he finally asked.

One of her eyebrows rose. Well, all right, maybe the whole world *didn't* know her. "No, of course not, Mr. Frederick." She took a deep breath. "Mr. Frederick, I write diet books and I'm as fat as a cow. My editor just called and told me I'm scheduled to go on *Mornings with Morton* in three weeks. Mr. Frederick, this is serious. I'll pay good money. Are you interested or aren't you?"

A soft chuckle emanated from the phone. At any other time, on any other day, in any other life, she'd have found it infinitely attractive. Today it grated along her nerve endings like sandpaper. He clucked at her, sounding like a mother hen. "Mrs. Daniels, you *do* have a problem."

"Tell me about it," she said wryly. "Well? Are you interested, or aren't you?"

"I'm interested."

"You are?" Her hopes soared. She would have kissed the man if he were here in the flesh. "Bless you, sir. May the sun always shine on your house and home. May the blue-bird—"

"Mrs. Daniels," he said dryly, breaking in. "When can we meet?"

"Whenever you say. The sooner the better. Now. Better yet, an hour ago."

"Can you come by in half an hour?"

"No, Mr. Frederick, you've got to come to me."

"I do?"

"You do. It's imperative. Essential. I can't be seen going to a fitness gym. I'd lose my credibility."

"How do you get along normally? I mean, surely you go out, go to church, buy groceries, gas for the car, that sort of thing."

"Uh-uh. I've just spent ten weeks writing a new book. When I write, I don't go anywhere. My groceries are delivered. They pull vans up to my back door and unload for hours. All I do is write, eat and sleep. It's totally disgusting. My grocer loves me. Before I moved to the Cape, he used to close in the off-season."

He didn't chuckle this time, but she was sure he was smiling. Somehow she could feel a smile coming through the phone lines at her. She herself smiled. "Well, okay, so maybe I exaggerate a little. I used to write for a comedian. Then I wised up and decided to write for myself. The ultimate comedy: the fat lady who writes successful diet books. Woody Allen couldn't do better himself."

He sighed, sounding oddly winsome. "Okay. But where do I go?"

"Mr. Frederick, you're a wonderful man. May life always be good to you. May you always—"

"Mrs. Daniels, where do you live?"

"Oh." Smiling, she gave him directions, then hung up. God, life was good. If only she had more Carnaby Chocolate Creams....

Kyle Frederick pulled his pickup to a stop and sat looking at Delta Daniels's house. It was big and impressive, one of those modern houses built to resemble a Cape Cod-style cottage, but lacking all its charm and warmth. The shingles hadn't even faded to silver yet, and instead of a white picket fence with rambler roses climbing over it, a low rock wall separated the clipped lawn from the field of seagrass. Beyond the marsh, the tranquil waters of Cape Cod Bay glittered in the midday sun.

Kyle climbed from the truck and slammed the door. He stretched his lean six-foot-two frame and hunched his shoulders under his faded chambray shirt, tilting his head to the side and back to loosen the tension. Sighing, he ran a hand through his tousled dirty-blond hair. Fine way for a former Olympic champion to be making a living—barking at fat ladies to make them lose weight.

He frowned to himself and started for the front door, remembering the warning of Harry Collins, the trainer who had dogged his every step ten years ago. "You retirin', Kyle?" Harry had asked, shaking his head mournfully. "I don't know. How you gonna cope? I seen too many former athletes gettin' soft and fat, livin' on the memory of their glory days. Retirement for an athlete's no good, Kyle. You'll get depressed, think you're a has-been." He'd leaned forward and almost whispered it: "You'll never do nothin' for the rest of your life that'll match winnin' the decathlon, Kyle." He'd shaken his head sadly. "Early success. It's a curse."

But, dammit, that wasn't what was bugging him. He could understand it if his identity were tied to his athletic achievements, but he'd never thought of himself as just Kyle Frederick, the Olympic champion. He was the son of Lewis and Hannah Frederick, brother of Luke and Mary, uncle of Jody and Jim. He was a transplanted resident of Cape Cod, a fitness trainer, operator of a local gym. But something enormously important was lacking in his life—a wife, children, the warmth of family life. He lived alone and was heartily sick of it, yet no woman he met ever measured up to what he wanted.

He pressed the doorbell, then turned his back to the front door and stood looking out toward the marshes that skirted the property. It was early April and unseasonably mild. The sky was a high bluish-white canopy with traces of cloud on the horizon. The water in the bay was deeper blue, rippled here and there by a playful curl of white surf. Daffodils nodded sleepily under a stand of birch, and chickadees chattered in the maples. He took a deep, satisfied breath, then turned at the sound of the door opening.

For a moment he was discombobulated. He'd expected an overweight woman with plump cheeks and a Cupid's bow mouth. Instead, he was looking at a face that would put Helen of Troy to shame. Large green eyes stared back at him. Disheveled dark brown hair curled in wild abandon around her face. She had a nose that tilted up slightly and a wide, strong mouth that was sensual enough to make his stomach curl and cause him to clear his throat. He noted the aqua sweatshirt and sweatpants straining at the seams and realized she'd bought them when she was two sizes smaller. Too bad about the extra pounds. Slim, she would be a knockout.

"Uh, I'm Kyle Frederick. I'm here to see Mrs. Daniels. I guess that'd be your mother. Is she here?"

Delta could only stare. He was beautiful, the kind of man you found on the pages of glossy magazines, the kind of man who made you drool. He had sandy blond hair and sparkling blue eyes and a square, solid chin that looked as if it had been chipped from a slab of granite. He was tall and lean with ruddy, healthy-looking skin and a mouth she would give ten years off her life to kiss. He wore a faded chambray shirt and even more faded jeans that rode low on his lean hips. Her eyes dipped and noticed the jogging shoes on his feet, then lifted again to his face, ignoring the hint of crisp blond chest hair that peeked from the open collar of his shirt.

"Delta Daniels," she said, finding her voice. "That's me."

"I expected someone older."

She shrugged, grinning. "I'm a child prodigy. I started writing when I was ten." Stepping back, she held open the door. "Come on in."

She led him down the Mexican clay-tiled hall into the shiny white Formica kitchen with its gleaming stainless-steel sink and stove, and a greenhouse addition that served as a dining area.

"Coffee?" she asked, pouring herself a cup.

"No thanks." He reached out and put a hand on hers and shook his head. "No sugar, Mrs. Daniels. It's not good for you."

"Oh." She nodded and dumped the sugar back into the bowl. "It's Ms. Daniels," she said. "And I'm not married." She sighed and sipped her coffee, then made a face. "You can see what you're up against. Sweets are my downfall. I'm a compulsive eater. Look at me: Tubby the Tuba personified."

He chuckled, the same chuckle she remembered from their phone conversation, but now it was even more appealing since it was combined with his face. She tilted her head and surreptitiously glanced at his left hand for a wedding band. She found none, but that didn't mean anything. There was some unwritten law somewhere: good-looking men never wore wedding bands.

She folded her arms and leaned back against the kitchen counter. "I need to lose at least twenty pounds in three weeks, Mr. Frederick. Can you do it?"

"That's the wrong question, Ms. Daniels. The question is, can *you* do it?"

"Yeah. I see what you mean." She frowned, then lifted her eyes. "Well? Can I?"

"How's your motivation?"

"First-rate," she said. "My editor'll kill me if I don't go on Bill Morton's show. On the other hand, if I go on fat, my readers and critics will kill me." She shrugged. "There's only one solution: lose weight. I guess you could say I'm motivated."

He nodded thoughtfully, his blue eyes skimming her figure. "How tall are you and how much do you weigh?"

She shuddered. "Don't ask."

"Ms. Daniels, if I'm going to be your trainer, I have to know these things."

She debated that, then shrugged. "Five-five. One-forty."

"You need to lose a good twenty to twenty-five pounds."

"I *know* that," she grumbled, "but what do you expect? Miracles? I've got three *weeks*, dammit, not three months!"

"All right, all right, don't get touchy." A hint of a smile played at the corners of his mouth. His blue eyes sparkled. "If I work with you, you'll have to agree to everything I say."

She looked at him out of the corner of her eye. "Oh?"

"*Oh*. I'll have complete say over your diet, your exercise, your social life—"

"Social life? Ha! I told you—I just finished writing a book and have been hibernating for ten weeks. Anyway, I only moved here last fall. The only people I know on the entire Cape are my grocer and my shrink."

"You're in counseling? That's good."

She shrugged. "That's what he says, but then he's getting rich off me."

"If I find you cheating on your diet once, Ms. Daniels— even once—we're finished. You're on your own."

She nodded, eyes wide. This guy was serious. Good, she needed that. Someone in her life had to be. "Okay, I promise. I swear it. I'll do whatever you say for the next three weeks. Let's shake on it."

"We're not finished negotiating, Ms. Daniels."

"We're not?"

"We're not. The fee."

"Oh, that." She waved away the words. "Name it. Any figure—no pun intended."

He named what seemed like an excessively high price.

She shrugged. She'd pay anything to lose this weight. "Okay."

He drew a piece of paper out of his back pocket. "I brought a contract with me, Ms. Daniels—"

"A contract? My, aren't we formal."

"I'm in business, Ms. Daniels. It's a precaution, that's all. I had it drawn up by a reputable lawyer and use it for all my customers. It stipulates that you won't hold me responsible for any physical damage incurred, that sort of thing."

"Physical damage..." She swallowed, then forced a smile. "Of course. How smart of you to think of that kind of thing."

He held a pen out to her. "Sign here, Ms. Daniels."

She took the pen, but hesitated. What did she know about this guy? He was big and tall and lean, though not muscle-bound. "You have any references?" she asked.

He pulled a card from his wallet and handed it to her. "Call any of these people. They're upstanding citizens here on the Cape who'll vouch for me. Or call the chamber of commerce, or Better Business Bureau."

She eyed the list of names. "Would you wait here while I call?"

At his quick nod, she went to her study and hurriedly dialed the first name on the list. "Kyle Frederick?" the man asked, laughing. "Yeah, I'd recommend him. He's about the best there is. Aside from knowing how to get the best out of people, ten years ago he won the decathlon at the Olympics. Guess you're not going to find anyone better."

Delta thanked him and hung up, feeling embarrassed. Suddenly, everything clicked into place. No wonder she'd thought his name seemed familiar. It had been buried in her gray matter with all the other trivia of the past ten years. Kyle Frederick had been a national hero for one summer ten years ago. As winner of the decathlon, he'd brought honor and fame to his country. She walked back to the kitchen.

"I should've known you," she said, looking embarrassed. "You were a hero."

He smiled and shook his head. "That was a long time ago, and not all that important." His smile turned to a grin. "Anyway, we're even. I should have known you, too."

She smiled, picked up the pen and signed her name. "It's a deal, Mr. Frederick."

Picking up the contract, he stared down at her name. "Delta. Odd name." He looked up and smiled, sending her stomach into orbit. "It's pretty, though. How'd you get it?"

"Typographical error," she said, smiling at the expression on his face.

"Oh," he said, laughing. "Another joke."

"Actually it isn't."

"You're kidding."

She laughed outright. "Nope. My mother named me Della when I was born, but the person who typed up the records in the hospital typed Delta and it got put on my birth certificate. My mother went on calling me Della and the official world went on knowing me as Delta. It wasn't until I went to nursery school that it all got ironed out. One of the teachers mentioned it to her and she laughed and shrugged and said, 'Oh. Well, Delta it is, I guess,' and that's how I got to be Delta."

She expected him to laugh. Everyone always did. It was a funny story the way she told it. But Kyle Frederick didn't laugh. Instead, he frowned, as if sensing the underlying meaning in her words.

"She didn't try to straighten it out and get it changed back to Della?" he asked.

Suddenly uncomfortable, Delta looked away from those puzzled eyes. "No," she said, "she didn't. She was going through one of her divorces then. I guess maybe that accounts for it...."

But of course it didn't. Not really. Long ago it had bothered her that her mother hadn't cared enough to notice a mistake on her birth certificate, much less correct it. Then Delta had learned that humor deflected pain, and slowly she'd gotten so good at telling the story for laughs that she'd almost forgotten how hurt she'd once been by it.

Now she shrugged off the memory and lifted sparkling green eyes. Everyone loved a clown—she'd learned that, too. "So," she said brightly. "When do we begin?"

Kyle Frederick folded the contract and slid it into his back jeans pocket. "Right now, Ms. Daniels."

"Thank you!" she exclaimed, folding her hands in prayer. "Bless you, Mr. Frederick. May you and your wife have a dozen fine sons to carry on your name. May you and she bask in their glories forever. May both of you—"

"Ms. Daniels," he said quietly. "I'm not married."

"Oh," she said, then the implication of his words sank in. "Oh." She swallowed, realizing she would be spending the next three weeks with this perfectly gorgeous, eligible man. Without thinking, she reached for a cookie. "Okay, where do we begin?"

"Here," he said, taking the cookie from her and throwing it down the garbage disposal.

"Oh." Darn it, she *hated* reality. It just wasn't fun at all.

Two

___

With her nose pressed to her bedroom window, Delta stared at Kyle Frederick as he walked toward his truck. He wasn't a man to waste time, that was for sure. He'd assured her that he had some gym clothes in his truck; all he had to do was change and they could begin. She'd tried to tell him that tomorrow was soon enough, but he'd said that today wasn't soon enough if she had to lose twenty pounds in three weeks.

Delta sighed wistfully as she watched him lean inside his pickup to get his clothes. What a body! If she needed incentive to lose weight, having a hunk like Kyle Frederick around should do the trick. Then she frowned. Of course, handsome men had never helped in the past. Every time she fell in love, she gained weight. Other women seemed to lose weight when they met attractive men, but good old Delta put on the pounds as if fat acted as an aphrodisiac. Every time she lost weight she met a new man, and every time she met a new man she gained weight until the man disappeared.

Her counselor had asked if there were a connection, but of course there wasn't. It was just her rotten luck, that was all.

Pushing the thought from her head, she shoved her hair back and slipped a headband over her forehead, then winced when she glimpsed herself in the full-length mirror. How could she have let herself gain all this weight? Hadn't she even looked at herself these past ten weeks? Hadn't she realized what was happening?

She tried to recall her mood during the past couple of months, but everything was a blur. When she wrote, she shut out the rest of the world. She lived in her study, writing from dawn to dusk, then researched new recipes for her diet in the kitchen at night. At midnight, after sampling the newly concocted dishes, she would crawl upstairs and tumble into bed, only to repeat the entire schedule the next day, then the next, until time became an undifferentiated whirl of days and nights.

Now, staring at herself in the mirror, she felt her self-esteem take a giant pratfall. She had been on this weight-loss roller coaster since she was nineteen years old, and every time she lost weight, she vowed she would never gain it back. But she *did* gain it back every time, and each time she did, she felt worse about herself. When she'd moved here to the Cape, she'd decided to start seeing a therapist—just about the only person she *had* been seeing—but so far he hadn't done her any good. All he'd done was sit and listen to her talk once a week. What was the matter with the guy? Why hadn't he warned her she was gaining weight these past ten weeks? Hadn't he seen what she was doing to herself?

Delta felt a huge surge of anger ripple through her, followed by an even larger wave of hunger. She looked around her bedroom. Hadn't she hidden a box of Carnaby's Chocolate Creams in here last month? She looked in her dresser drawers and peered into the closet, went down on her knees and searched under the bed, but she couldn't find one. Oh, well, there were cookies downstairs. Just one cookie wouldn't hurt her. After all, Kyle Frederick had said they would start by going jogging. She was sure to run off the calories from one cookie in the first quarter mile....

Humming breezily, Delta sailed into the kitchen, then stopped short. All the cabinet doors were open, and Kyle Frederick was emptying the shelves of all food, stuffing packages of cookies and cake mixes and brownies into paper bags and boxes.

"What are you *doing*?" she cried.

He glanced over his shoulder and smiled. "You're going on a diet, remember? You won't be needing this stuff. I'll take it all over to the soup kitchen at the church later on, after our jog."

"I—" Delta broke off as she watched him transfer two bags of potato chips and a bag of pretzels to a box on the floor. "Wait a minute," she wailed. "You're cleaning me out of house and home!"

"That's right," he said affably. "Any objections?"

She felt her heart sink at the sight of all those goodies being removed from her kitchen, then she lifted her gaze and forced a smile. "Why, no," she said, knowing she sounded as enthusiastic as a cheerleader after the team had lost the big game. "It's just...you surprised me, that's all. I mean..." She shrugged, laughing weakly. "You're thorough—very thorough."

"If you're serious about losing weight, there's only one way I know to do it—cold turkey. You can't ease into a weight loss campaign, Ms. Daniels. You have to jump right in. The sooner you accustom yourself to no snacks and eight hundred calories, the better off you'll be."

"Eight hundred calories!" Delta wailed. "Eight hundred calories is what I snack on midmorning! I have a few doughnuts or a pastry or two, and a couple cups of coffee just for a snack."

"From now on you'll have melba toast, if you're lucky. Actually, you should eat a small apple or pear."

"Apples!" Delta made a face. "I hate 'em. The skin's too hard to chew."

"How do you feel about pears?"

"Ugh!"

"Maybe I should have charged twice as much," Kyle said, sighing. "You're going to be a challenge."

Delta stared at him, feeling reality intrude even further into her consciousness. The next three weeks were going to be hell. Even the company of a hunk like Kyle Frederick wouldn't compensate for the loss of her beloved pastries and candy bars. "Maybe I should just take my editor up on her suggestion," she said tiredly.

"What's that?"

"She offered to come out here and sew my mouth shut."

Kyle Frederick caught himself just in time and was able to keep from laughing. "It's not that bad, Ms. Daniels," he said gently. "Maybe we should get out of the kitchen and do something to get your mind off food."

"Like what?" she asked, feeling suddenly listless. "What could possibly take my mind off food?"

"Jogging," he said, and broke into a grin at the expression that crossed her face when he said the word.

"Jogging!"

"Precisely. Don't look so discouraged, Ms. Daniels, you're going to love it. But before we start, I think you should tell me if you have any physical problems I should be aware of."

Gamely Delta forced a smile. "I had a physical last month; I'm as healthy as a horse." Then she really did forget about food, for Kyle reached out and took her arm, and when he did, her stomach did a complete flip and her mouth went dry. *Now* how was she going to manage? It was bad enough that she didn't have her blessed food to comfort her. Now she had to contend with her attraction to the best-looking man she'd ever seen.

"Normally, I'd have you start out slowly," Kyle said, jogging easily alongside Delta, "but since your check-up was good and we've got so little time, I'm going to skip a few levels."

"I," she puffed, "see...." A river of sweat rolled down Delta's face and trickled into the valley between her considerable breasts. Running, she felt as if she were toting two bags of cantaloupe on her chest. Her sweatshirt was soaked and her hair was in unbecoming ringlets around her face. Her legs had long ago decided to feel like lead, her lungs were bursting, and there was that pain in her side that wouldn't go away, but other than that she was doing just fine on her first jog.

"How," she puffed again, "much...farther?"

"Oh, another couple of miles or so ought to do it."

"A..." Huff-puff-huff-puff-huff-puff. "Another..." God, she was hyperventilating! No, she was dying. She was already in the damned tunnel they always talked about, the one with the light at the end. She trotted to a stop, chest heaving, sweat trickling, lungs bursting. "Miles?" she asked between puffs. "Did you say *miles*?"

"Walk, Ms. Daniels," Kyle instructed, jogging around her in easy circles. "Keep moving."

She nodded, bent double. "I'll walk when my heart tells me it's okay."

"Your heart's getting a good workout, Ms. Daniels, probably for the first time in years, but it'll be just fine if you continue to walk. Stopping cold like that is a shock to the body."

If he thought *stopping* was a shock to the body, he would be amazed at what the thought of starting up again was. Delta straightened, readjusting the damp sweatband. "Okay," she said, her breathing more normal now. "I'll walk for a while."

"Good. You're starting to burn all kinds of calories, Ms. Daniels. That little engine inside is revving up and beginning to devour them."

"Don't tell me about my little engine, Mr. Frederick," Delta retorted. "My little engine is tottering along on one cylinder."

"Just thought you'd like to know what's happening," Kyle said, grinning as he jogged beside her. "Think you're up to a slow jog again?"

"Mr. Frederick, I won't be up to a slow jog for at least another year."

"Try it anyway," he said.

Obediently she tried it, managing a passable imitation of a shuffling jog. "When I get home," she said between huge gulps of air, "I'm going to eat an entire barnyard. Chickens, cows, pigs—you name it, I'll devour it."

"No, Ms. Daniels, you're not."

She slowed to a walk. "I'm not? What am I going to eat?"

"I'm putting you on a very strict eight-hundred-calorie, low-fat, low-cholesterol diet the first week. If you lose weight, I'll up it to a thousand calories."

"You don't seem to understand, Mr. Frederick," Delta said. "I'm in danger of fainting if I don't get something to eat very soon. We've got to ease into this dieting thing. Let me at least have some carbohydrates for supper. Some spaghetti, maybe, or lasagna with a little cheese." She sighed and mentally licked her chops. "And sausage and peppers and three or four pieces of garlic bread . . ."

"Salad, Ms. Daniels," Kyle said. "That's what you'll have for supper tonight. Tossed salad, with low-cal dressing and raw vegetables. You're on a diet, remember?"

"The problem with dieting, Mr. Frederick, is it removes all reason for living." Delta speeded herself up to a moderate jog again, secretly amazed she hadn't passed out yet. "Food is life's greatest joy, its only comfort. Going without it is like sentencing yourself to prison."

"Yet you write diet books."

"I'm an expert on diets," she said dryly. "I've been on one all my adult life."

"Yet they obviously don't work."

She winced. "Don't say that, Mr. Frederick. I can hear my book sales plummeting now."

"Have you ever tried exercising along with dieting?"

"Mr. Frederick, that's like asking a person if they've tried going without shelter as well as going without food. Dieting's bad enough. Why compound the agony by exercising?"

"Because it means you have to diet less."

She trotted to a stop and bent over, struggling to control her breathing. "Have we jogged enough yet?"

"Keep walking, Delta. Stopping cold like that is strictly forbidden. We've got another mile to do at least."

She harrumphed to herself, but did as she was told, falling behind Kyle Frederick as he jogged ahead. In her scheme of things, the only thing worse than going without food was exercising, yet for the next three weeks, she would have to do both.

Her eyes slid down Kyle's masculine frame, taking in the hard muscles that rippled rhythmically in his legs and arms. His jogging shorts were almost indecent, but she wasn't going to complain. She couldn't remember the last time she'd been this close to such a good-looking man. Not that it would do her any good. At 140 pounds she was hardly the kind of woman a man like Kyle Frederick would be interested in.

She grinned sardonically, remembering the long line of hunks who had paraded through her life, all paying tribute to her beautiful half sister. Delta herself had been slim once, but when she had brought her first real boyfriend home from college he'd fallen for Sheila. That was when Delta had started gaining weight. She'd been so angry she hadn't stopped eating for a month. When she did stop, she was fat, and she'd been that way ever since, give or take the fifteen or twenty times she'd lost weight before gaining it right back.

"Jog, Delta!"

Kyle Frederick's shouted command invaded her thoughts. She groaned and rolled her eyes, then put herself into forward gear and pushed her tired muscles into action. It was going to be a long three weeks.

She caught up with Kyle as they were approaching her house. Heart thumping erratically, chest heaving, sweat soaking her sweatshirt, Delta wasn't in any shape for casual conversation, but Kyle wasn't even out of breath.

"How'd you get started writing diet books?" he asked easily.

She groaned. "Don't remind me about them. If I didn't write them, I wouldn't be in this mess. But to answer your question, I wrote the first one on a lark. I was living in New York, writing comedy routines for a comedy show. I'd gone on a diet and lost about thirty pounds. Someone joked that I should write a book and get rich, and one day I decided to give it a try. When I'd finished it, I gave it to my agent, and she sent it to a publisher, and the rest is history." Delta laughed. "That was a darned good diet. Only trouble is, once you've lost and gained weight a few times, it gets harder and harder to lose, so I keep having to come up with new diets. Of course, that pleases my publisher no end, so I stopped writing comedy and began writing diet books full-time."

"So you really did used to write comedy routines. You weren't just joking."

"I wasn't joking." Delta peered at Kyle, but he was busy stretching. Her eyes ran down the hard length of his sinewed legs, and she felt herself grow dizzy. Must be all that running, she thought, beginning the stretching routine he'd taught her before they began their jog.

"Have you always been overweight?" he asked.

"No. When I was a kid, I was pretty skinny, actually."

"What happened? Why'd you gain weight?"

She hesitated, keeping her eyes on her legs as she did her cool-down routine. "I put a lot of weight on one year, and I've never been the same since," she said.

"Oh? Any particular reason?"

She looked up and found him watching her. She shook her head. "No. Why do you ask?"

"Because there's often an underlying reason why people gain weight. Of course, often the pounds just creep up, especially with women, but you said you put it all on in one year.''

Dammit, when would she learn to keep her mouth shut? If she didn't get into trouble by shoving food into it, she got into trouble by talking too much.

"Being overweight is sometimes a defense, too,'' Kyle was saying. His eyes narrowed as he watched her.

She lifted her head. "Oh?"

"Mmm-hmm.'' He shrugged. "Of course, sometimes it's glandular or related to health problems. Sometimes it's just the result of the body's natural slowing of metabolism, but a lot of times it's emotional. But since you're 'healthy as a horse,' as you put it, we can concentrate on working you as hard as possible these next three weeks.''

She met his eyes, refusing to look away. "You think I'm going to cave in, don't you? You think I'm going to fink out on you. Well, I won't, Mr. Frederick. Losing this weight means too much to me.''

He pulled his sweaty singlet over his head and wadded it into a ball. "I'm wondering if I'm not wasting my time, Delta. You may lose the weight, but are you going to keep it off? That's what I'm interested in.''

She tried to keep her eyes off his chest, tried to keep her mouth from feeling so inexplicably dry. "That's my business, isn't it?''

"No, Delta, it's mine. I believe in fitness. I've made a career out of it. I don't want to spend the next three weeks working with you, only to have you throw it all away once you've finished appearing on television.''

She turned her back, busying herself with retying her jogging shoes. "Is that what you think? Why does it bother you what I look like?''

"You're a very lovely woman, Delta. You could be a knockout if you slimmed down. I should think you'd care very much about how you look.''

She went very still, then slowly lifted her gaze from her shoes and stared at the ground unseeingly. Suddenly her fingers were trembling and her stomach was swirling. She took a deep breath and turned around. "You seem to be saying that I'm not attractive the way I am now."

"Not as attractive as you could be, no."

"I really dislike it when people judge a person by her looks," she said quietly. "Everything is reduced to how she looks, to whether she could be on the cover of the swimsuit issue of *Sports Illustrated*."

"A lot of overweight people feel that way, but it's hardly a reason for remaining overweight."

"No? Maybe we just like the thought of being wanted for ourselves, not our bodies."

"Or perhaps you don't want to have to deal with the possibility of being wanted at all."

She stared at him, then burst out laughing. "Hey! I just like food, okay? I mean, I love the stuff. Why do we have to get Freudian here? I'll do my best to keep the weight off. I'll diet and exercise and take my editor's advice and sew my mouth shut, okay? Will that please you?"

He shrugged a shoulder. "That sounds fine."

Delta took a ragged breath, dragged off her headband and shook back her hair. "God, I could go for a nice chocolate milk shake right now."

Kyle laughed and shook his head. "I can see you're going to be more than a handful."

She grinned, turned on her heel and walked toward her house. They were on solid ground again, not talking about being attractive to the opposite sex or any of that garbage. Honestly, she thought, sometimes men dreamed up the silliest explanations for weight gain. This Kyle Frederick—he sounded exactly like her therapist....

Delta walked into the kitchen after her shower to find Kyle preparing a salad. She came to a stop, her head tilted to one side as she dried her hair. "Hey, what are you doing?"

"Fixing supper," Kyle said, not even bothering to look at her.

"Is this part of your fee?" she asked, smiling.

"Uh-huh," he said, answering her smile with a grin. "Three weeks from today I want you to look like Bo Derek." He picked up a piece of cauliflower and shook it at her. "And this is gonna do the trick." He opened the refrigerator door and peered inside, then held up a bottle of blue cheese dressing and shook his head disapprovingly. "Write down low-cal dressing on that list over there, will you?"

"I don't like low-cal dressing," she protested. "It tastes like water."

"Fine, then go without. That's even better."

She threw her towel on a chair and put her hands on her hips. "I'm not sure I like this, Mr. Frederick."

"Oh, call me Kyle. We're going to be old friends by the time the next three weeks are finished." He put the salad ingredients into a plastic bag and stuck them in the refrigerator. "Ready?"

"For what?"

"We're going to drop these off at the soup kitchen, then go grocery shopping."

"Grocery shopping?" Delta began to laugh. "Well, if that doesn't beat all! You just cleaned me out of a month's supply of food, and now you want to take me grocery shopping."

He picked up a half pound of Brie. "Loaded with calories," he said, then pointed to a stick of summer sausage. "Filled with fat. This kind of food will put the pounds on faster than I could take them off you." He lifted a box and headed for the door. "Come on, Delta, don't just stand there. A little carrying will be good for you."

She stood and stared, openmouthed. Dammit, she'd been happy before Marcia called about appearing on *Mornings with Morton*. Personally she didn't think appearing on a silly television show warranted all this trouble.

Three

———

At six the next morning Delta opened one eye and peered at the clock next to her bed. What was that godawful pounding? She snuggled under her blankets, trying to ignore the sound. Then she realized it was someone at her back door.

"Who the...?" Bounding out of bed, she threw her robe around herself and hurried downstairs. She parted the curtains and stared.

Kyle Frederick stared back at her. Delta looked down at herself and uttered a low groan. She looked like a whale in a pink silk nightgown with lace trim. Tying the belt of her robe more securely around her middle, she opened the door.

"Morning," Kyle said, smiling. "Looks like I woke you."

"How could you tell," she grumbled. Her hair stood out around her head like Brillo, and she would bet any money that her face had those ugly creases that always occurred when she slept on her stomach and pressed her face into the pillows. She wouldn't allow herself to think about how her lush body looked under the sheer pink silk nightgown.

Kyle Frederick didn't seem to mind thinking along those lines, though. His blue eyes were surreptitiously sweeping over her, and she got the distinct impression he liked what he saw. Which was total nonsense! Sure, Delta had heard the rumors that some men liked women with a little flesh on their bones, but the amount of flesh on *her* bones made a Perdue chicken look scrawny. Then she realized the plunging collar of her robe hid little of her magnificent décolletage from his inquisitive eyes. She nonchalantly pulled the collar of her robe together.

"So," she said, clearing her throat. "You're here early."

"No," he said. "I'm right on time."

She blinked. "You are?"

"Mmm-hmm." He flung his jacket on a chair and ran water into the tea kettle. "I'll get breakfast while you get dressed. Wear something warm—it's chilly out there."

"Out where?" She tried to pull her eyes off his back, but it was difficult. He wore a T-shirt and sweatpants, and Delta found herself staring fixedly at the muscles in his upper body and arms. Every time he moved his arms, the muscles rippled sensually, and her stomach did a funny little two-step. And as for his tush, it was magnificent. She would give anything to see him without his clothes on....

Startled, she raised stricken eyes and saw that he was grinning at her. "Like what you see?" he asked matter-of-factly.

Red-faced, she half stammered, half laughed. "I...you...ha..." Turning, she fled.

"Going somewhere?" Kyle called after her.

"I'll be right down," she called over her shoulder, hoping he couldn't hear the embarrassment in her voice. "I just have to get dressed."

When she came downstairs again, she found Kyle buried behind the morning paper, sipping black coffee from a heavy white mug, an empty cereal bowl pushed toward the center of the table.

"What's for breakfast?" she asked, pulling out a chair. She had visions of scrambled eggs and rashers of bacon, and

English muffins dripping with butter and marmalade. Wasn't that how fighters in training ate?

He shoved a cup of steaming hot water toward her and said, "Bottoms up."

She stared at the cup, then chuckled. "I'm so glad you've got a sense of humor, Kyle. I mean, I've known fitness freaks who never even *laugh*, you know?" She rolled her eyes and pulled a box of cereal toward her, but he reached out and touched her arm.

"Uh-uh," he said in a light, singsong voice, pointing at the cup of hot water. "It's got lemon in it. Great natural diuretic, hot water and lemon."

She eyed him with disbelief. "You're kidding."

"Nope. You drink that, then we'll run a few miles, then come back and do calisthenics. By the way, I'm moving some weight training equipment in later this morning. I checked out your rec room—it'll go perfect there."

"Do you mean to sit there and tell me you expect me to drink hot water and *lemon*?"

"Sure do." He folded the paper and stood up. "Now, Delta."

His voice had taken on a slight edge, as if he were losing patience with her. She stared at him belligerently, then picked up the cup and sipped from it. She made a face. "This is *horrible*!"

"Most things are that are good for you," he said, shrugging.

She glared at him. "I need food," she said coldly. "My blood sugar's so low I'll faint if I go out running on an empty stomach."

"I doubt it, Delta," he said in a knowing voice. "Drink up. Time's a-wastin'." He folded his arms, and she wondered if he'd done it to draw her attention to them.

"This is not fun," she said stonily.

"It's not meant to be. It's meant to help you lose those twenty pounds in twenty days."

She stared at him, then looked down at the steaming hot water and lemon. If she ever got through this, she decided, she would never write another diet book as long as she lived.

"Seventeen, eighteen, nineteen," said Kyle, counting as Delta did her sit-ups. Sweat streamed down her face and formed a dark, damp patch on her sweatshirt front, but she struggled up, knees bent, hands clasped behind her head, mouth set in a firm line, teeth clenched.

"Breathe, Delta," Kyle said.

She let out a pent-up breath and collapsed back on the exercise mat. It was only ten o'clock, but they had already jogged four miles. Now the slave master was standing over her with a metaphorical whip, egging her on to side-splitting exercise. At this rate, she would lose fifty pounds in a week.

"Sit up, Delta," Kyle commanded. "Your goal is thirty sit-ups today. Keep going."

Awkwardly she pushed herself up, her body straining to raise itself against the push of inertia—or was that the pull of gravity? She began to shake, and her body stopped midway up, trembling, her elbows halfway to her bent knees, her back rounded, her face red with exertion and wet with sweat. "I can't," she gasped.

"You can. One more. Try, Delta, try."

"I can't."

"You can. You can do it, Delta. One more. Come on, honey, don't give up. You can do it, Delta. Try. One more."

She gave it everything she had and miraculously pulled herself up, feeling her trembling muscles ease and an unbearable weight drop off her shoulders.

"Great! You did it!"

Shakily she began to laugh. Exhilaration and pride were racing through her bloodstream, sending her newfound strength, both mental and physical.

"Come on, now, ten more, Delta. That's only twenty."

"But—"

"No buts. Come on, Delta, keep going."

She set her mouth in a rigid line, anger fueling her. Defiantly she uncurled and lay back on the mat, then forced herself up again, struggling, red-faced, determined to do it. It took her almost five minutes, but she did the final ten sit-ups, then lay back on the mat, exhausted.

"Delta, you're doing great," Kyle said, standing over her.

She closed her eyes. She refused to look at him. He was cruel and unusually punishing.

"Come on, Delta," he said. "You're almost done. Just go through the cool-down segment."

"Cool down, schmool down," she muttered. "I'd rather cool off this way."

Unceremoniously Kyle hauled her to her feet. "Stretch out," he commanded, "then hit the shower."

"You're a bully!" she cried.

He arched a wry brow and tapped her fanny with a yardstick. "Uh-huh."

Without a word, she sat down with her back to him and began doing the cool-down exercises. She didn't look up when he approached her.

"Look," he said quietly. "I know you're mad at me, but this is what you hired me for."

She kept her eyes straight ahead, but began to count out loud. "Three, four, five..."

"Delta."

"Seven, eight..."

"Delta, look at me."

She stopped counting and just sat there, one leg stretched out before her, the other bent at the knee.

"Delta," he said, his voice low and coaxing. "Look at me. Please."

She considered his request, fighting internally with herself, then reluctantly did as he asked. He was incredibly close, she realized, so close she could see the shadow of his beard and smell the faint aroma of after-shave mingled with the healthy scent of male sweat. She took an unsteady breath and tried to control the sudden clamor of her heart.

He reached out and tucked a wayward curl behind her ear. "You're doing just great, Delta," he said gently. "I know it's hard, but you've got to stick with it. In less than twenty-four hours, I'll bet you've already lost a couple of pounds. I think you can do it, Delta. I really think you can."

She stared into his eyes, feeling sudden hope burgeon within her. At least that's what she thought was sweeping through her on a fiery tide. She tried to speak, but for some reason her voice wouldn't work. Instead, she just kept sitting there, staring into his marvelous blue eyes, feeling dizzy and dazzled and more alive than she'd felt in years.

"You're so pretty, Delta," he said in a low voice.

She shivered at the way his breath whispered over her skin, and tried to suppress the giddy awareness of him that washed over her. The trouble was, he was just too attractive. He wasn't just good-looking; he was also magnetic. He had the kind of eyes that mesmerized a woman, making it impossible for her to look away. She felt a delicious spasm deep in her midsection that curled around and around like a pinwheel, making her feel astonishingly sexy. Suddenly she felt her nipples begin to pucker at the thought of his nearness. Oh, dear. Complications...

She stood up so fast she almost fell over, and Kyle had to reach out and steady her with a strong hand. "Um..." She licked her lips and stared at the brawny hand on her wrist. "Um... guess I better take a shower."

"Right," he said, staring into her eyes.

She backed away a step, then paused, gesturing absently. "I'll... um... be right back... after my shower...."

"Right."

She took an unsteady breath, then turned and floated from the room. In her mind she was already 110 pounds of lean, mean woman. She was svelte and firm and didn't jiggle when she walked. She was a definite size eight, and maybe even a six. And, by gosh, she just *loved* the way she felt!

* * *

When she came back downstairs from showering and changing into a red sweatshirt and sweatpants, Delta found Kyle and two muscle-bound men setting up huge stainless-steel pieces of weight-lifting equipment in her rec room just off the kitchen. She stood in the doorway, watching three magnificent male bodies in prime shape lift and shove and move those massive pieces of equipment, and she felt new hope. Maybe Kyle was right; maybe this time she could do it. Maybe this time she would lose the weight and keep it off. Maybe she would finally get the monkey off her back. She didn't want to think about it, but maybe there was a chance that this time she would make a go of a relationship with a man. A man like Kyle for instance. . . .

Pushing that thought from her head, she turned back to the kitchen and surveyed the pristine white Formica-covered cabinets, knowing that Kyle had thoroughly emptied them of all fattening foods. She was left with vegetables and fruit and little else. Restlessly she wandered toward the cabinets. She could use a snack, just a little something to assuage the hunger pangs, something crunchy, like potato chips. Opening every cabinet door, she was confronted with vacant shelves. He'd even removed the pasta. There wasn't anything worth snacking on, nothing oozy or creamy, nothing snappy or crunchy. It was disgusting.

She slammed the cabinet door and turned to find Kyle leaning against the doorframe, arms folded, one corner of his mouth lifted in amusement.

"Looking for something?" he asked casually.

"No," she said, just as casually, and wandered toward the refrigerator. "Just admiring the job you did cleaning out my cabinets."

"Uh-huh."

Why didn't he sound convinced? Smiling cheerily, she opened the refrigerator and peered inside. She had never had such a clean—or empty—refrigerator in her entire life. The shelves actually sparkled. She pulled open a crisper drawer and was greeted by pale green stalks of celery, freshly washed and nestled on top of a pile of McIntosh apples and some pears. She closed the door and turned to him.

"So," she said. "You guys get that exercise equipment moved in?"

"Sure did. It's all set up and waiting for you."

She nodded distractedly and opened the refrigerator door again, frowning as she checked the other crisper drawer. Lettuce—acres of the stuff. Fresh mushrooms, cucumbers, bright cherry tomatoes. Carrots. Irritably she grabbed one, bit off half, then shoved the drawer shut and slammed the door behind her.

"Good, huh?" Kyle asked, smiling broadly.

"Magnificent," she said dryly. "Like chewing leather."

"Well," he said, pushing away from the door frame and checking his watch, "it's almost time for lunch. I'll just subtract that carrot from your lunch calories and you'll still be on target for the day."

"Subtract—!" She stared at him, wide-eyed. "You're kidding," she said finally, beginning to laugh incredulously. "Subtract a *carrot* from my lunch calories?" As she gathered speed, her voice rose in volume until at last she was shaking the half-devoured carrot stick at him: "You're stark raving mad!"

Paying no attention, he merely penciled in the calorie count of a single carrot on her diet sheet and went about making her salad for lunch. "When I'm not here, Delta," he said, breaking lettuce leaves into a bowl, "make sure you record every single thing you eat. It's incredible how easy it is to go over the calorie limit on a diet. I'll bet you didn't even know you were going to eat that carrot stick when you opened the refrigerator. You eat automatically, the way other people breathe."

Startled, she stopped chomping on the carrot and stared at him. "Well, thanks a lot," she said sarcastically. "You make me sound like the fat woman at the circus."

He turned slowly, his face serious. "I'm sorry, Delta, I know you're sensitive about your weight, but we've got to be direct about the facts. You can tiptoe around them all you want, but that won't change the situation.''

"Why don't you just come out and say it?" she asked, her voice trembling slightly. "Why don't you just call me fat and leave it at that?"

"Because you're not fat," he said. "Technically, according to the new weight standards, for your height you're about ten to fifteen pounds overweight. That hardly makes you obese."

"Ten or fifteen—" She began to laugh, but he cut her off.

"That's right, Delta. You're a healthy, physically attractive woman, with a few excess pounds." He tilted his head consideringly. "But you don't realize that, do you? You hover between extremes. One moment you think you're hopelessly fat and unattractive, and the next you pretend that eating another cupcake won't hurt you. What you need, Delta, is a little straight, unbiased and objective feedback. Well, I can give it to you."

"Can you," she said, smiling tightly. "Is that included in your fee?"

He stood with his head angled to the side as he looked at her his eyes narrowed, a hint of a smile on his lips. "Yeah," he breathed softly, "it is."

She felt as if her breath had been suddenly knocked out of her, but all he was doing was leaning back against the kitchen counter, looking sexier than a man had a right to look. "I see," she said, then took a surreptitious deep breath. It wouldn't do to let on that he affected her. "Well . . ." She began to wander the kitchen distractedly, suddenly conscious of her hair, her posture, the way that damned stomach of hers tended to protrude. "I'm glad, Kyle," she said. "I'm really glad. I mean, if what you say is true—"

"It's true, all right," he said. "All you need to do is lose fifteen pounds, but I still think we should shoot for twenty. Firmed up and twenty pounds slimmer, you'll be fantastic looking, Delta."

"Oh?" She came to a stop three paces away from him. Keeping her eyes down, she pretended to be absorbed in a spot on the kitchen counter. "Why is that?" She knew her voice sounded breathless, but she couldn't help it. Something was coming; she could feel it. She lifted her head and turned to face Kyle. Her eyes met his, and she felt sparks go off, radiating around them like fireworks on the Fourth of July. Suddenly she felt weak and liquidy, as if all her muscles had melted and her bones had dissolved. It was his eyes that did it to her, she decided hazily—the admiring light in the deep blue depths, the way they looked so gentle, so warm, so... hot-blooded.

"You're beautiful, Delta," he said in a low voice.

Everything in her converged toward him, as if he were metal and she a magnet. It had been a long time since she'd felt this way. She'd almost forgotten the magical quality engendered by physical attraction. She felt as if she were drifting on a cloud of sweet light, soaring amid celestial music. She wasn't fat any longer, not unappealing. She was soft and sweet smelling and filled with longing. She was a woman, and Kyle Frederick was very much a man.

He reached out and touched the wayward curl near her ear, sending shivers cascading over her skin. "I don't think it's just Kyle Frederick the personal trainer you need," he said, his voice low and sounding strangely husky, as if he were affected by her as much as she was by him.

She lifted dazed eyes. "I don't?" She stared up at him, growing dizzy with longing. "What do you mean?"

He brushed his thumb softly against her cheek. "I think you need Kyle Frederick the man just as much," he murmured.

She stared at him, fighting the waves of attraction that passed between them. Stubbornly she pulled away, cutting the magnetic field. "Are you saying I just need a man, Mr. Frederick?" she asked icily. "A little tumble in the hay and all my weight problems will be solved?" She turned and put her back to him, feeling wounded. "I suppose you're willing to volunteer?" she asked coldly.

He turned her around, his hands strong but gentle on her arms. "I'm not saying you need just any man, Delta Daniels," he said. "I'm saying you need me."

She stared up at him, conflicting emotions warring within her. She felt herself sliding under his spell again, but she fought it, trying to hold on to the anger she'd felt just moments ago. "I know I need you, Mr. Frederick," she said, trying to sound normal, not out of breath like a yearning, hot-blooded woman. "That's why I hired you."

"Stop it, Delta," he said, his eyes boring into her. "This is no time for games."

"I don't know what you mean...." She tried to inch backward, but she ran into the hard edge of the kitchen counter.

It was no use; she was cornered. He was right—she *did* need him. Needed his strong arms and muscled body, needed his warmth and the nourishment that only a man's body could provide.

"I think you *do* know, Delta," he said, fastening a strong hand on the kitchen counter on either side of her and leaning toward her until his face was only inches from hers. "From the moment you opened your door yesterday, I found you attractive. Normally I make it a policy not to get involved with my clients, but you're different, Delta."

"I am?" She was getting breathless again.

He nodded, his eyes warm as he looked at her. "You joke and make sarcastic remarks all the time, but every time you do, I get this fierce urge to take you in my arms and just hold you."

"You do?" she whispered, her eyes wide.

"I do." He raised a gentle hand and brushed his knuckles back and forth across her cheek. "I get this urge to protect you, Delta."

She let out a tiny, wistful sigh and felt her eyes close. His hand went around the back of her neck, and he began to massage her tense muscles.

"I'm not going to rush you, Delta," he murmured, his lips just brushing her earlobe. "I'm going to let you take as long as you need to get used to me," he whispered, nuzzling the soft skin just under her ear. "But I want you to know it isn't all work for me. I'm not just here because you hired me, Delta. You could fire me tomorrow, or right now for that matter, and I'd still be back."

She groaned softly and felt herself melting into his strong arms, felt the glorious crescendo of pleasure spiral inside her as her body touched his, then he surprised her. He bent and kissed her cheek, then stood back and turned away from her.

"Where are you going?" she asked, startled that he'd stopped.

"I told you, Delta," he said, looking back at her. "I'm not going to rush you." One corner of his mouth lifted in a smile. "I'm going to finish making your lunch, though, then we're going to hit the Nautilus equipment and I'll show you how to use it. Every other day lifting weights, Delta, combined with everything else you're doing, and in three weeks you'll look like Miss America."

Delta took a tremulous breath and told herself to calm down. All that physical closeness had taken a lot out of her. Just thinking about getting involved with Kyle Frederick set her nerves fluttering.

Suddenly she was back in college, bringing home her first real boyfriend to meet her family, excited and in love, and filled with zest and eagerness. She saw it happening all over again, just as it had that day thirteen years earlier—the way Jack Peterson's eyes had lit up when he had spied her beautiful half sister, Sheila. Sheila's eyes had lit up as well. The next thing she knew Jack was sitting like a puppy at Sheila's feet, and Delta was forgotten.

Back in her own kitchen again, Delta swallowed painfully. She needed to eat something, fast. A cookie, maybe, or a piece of cake. Piece of cake, hell, she thought as her eyes devoured Kyle's muscular back. She needed an entire cake. Maybe even two or three.

Groaning inwardly, Delta acknowledged the truth yet again—it was going to be an *incredibly* long three weeks.

Four

Weight training will slim you down real quick if you stick with an every-other-day program," Kyle said, his hands on his hips as he stared down at Delta. She was lying on her back on a narrow board, gripping the handholds of the weight equipment, ready to lift twenty pounds ten times.

"The secret," he continued, "is in the way you breathe and the way you lift smoothly. No jerking the weights up. Lift easily and smoothly, keeping in correct position." He checked that her knees were bent and the flat of her back pressed into the board beneath her. "Okay, Delta, go to it."

Delta pulled down on the handles and felt the weights lift on their pulley system. "Hey," she exclaimed. "This is easy!"

"Don't get carried away, honey," Kyle said, grinning. "Just continue lifting in the same rhythm. Easy does it."

His calling her honey almost shook her, but she concentrated on the task at hand. By eight reps, Delta was beginning to feel the strain in her arm muscles. What had seemed simple now was beginning to seem a little harder. She took a deeper breath and paused, but Kyle was right there, cautioning her.

"Don't stop, Delta, keep up the pace. Nice and easy."

"But they're heavier," she said accusingly. "You must have added another ten pounds."

"It just feels that way. That's the purpose of the reps. Anyone can lift ten or twenty pounds. It's lifting it repeatedly that gets difficult."

Delta was ready for a rest when she finished her ten reps, but Kyle led her to the next piece of equipment, instructing her in how to stand in front of it and pull down on the handles, explaining what muscle groups this machine isolated, and how those muscles, properly worked, would contribute to a leaner, slimmer-looking Delta.

For the next half an hour, Kyle directed her around the circuit of equipment, patiently explaining, cautioning, cheering her on, then, ultimately, praising her.

"That's terrific, Delta. You've caught on beautifully."

She stared at him listlessly, her leotard wet with sweat, her chest heaving. "I thought this wasn't supposed to be aerobic exercise," she said, puffing.

"It's not, but when a person's as out of shape as—" He broke off, but Delta wouldn't let him off the hook so easily.

"Go ahead, Kyle, finish it," she said dryly. "When a person's as out of shape as me, any form of exercise is aerobic, eh?"

He grinned at her. "That's about it, Delta."

She wiped her brow with a towel, then slumped against the wall. "When can I weigh myself? I feel as if I've lost ten pounds already."

"You'll weigh in once a week. I don't want you to get distracted by the way the scale seems to hover at one-forty."

"Yeah," she said, nodding glumly. "It's the worst. In all my diet books, I caution my readers not to get discouraged. Fat is incredible. It sticks like Krazy Glue. Sometimes I think I could eat ten sticks of celery a day and gain weight." She lifted inquisitive eyes to Kyle. "Why is that? *Are* the gods crazy, or just vengeful?"

"It's just a little trick of nature, Delta. Fat cells grow more easily than other cells, and to make matters worse, they hold on to their fat harder, so it's a vicious cycle. The more you eat, the fatter you get, the fatter you get, the harder it is to lose weight."

"God is definitely a spoilsport," she remarked. "He must have been miffed on the sixth day and decided to make life miserable for women."

"It happens to men, too."

"Ha! Show me a man who has trouble controlling his weight the way a woman does."

"Okay, come on down to my gym. Watch the way those guys work out before they dare to down a cool brew at the local pub." Kyle shook his head. "Life's tough, Delta. No one said it'd be easy."

She tilted her chin up, her eyes filled with insolence. "It's easy for you, I'll bet," she taunted softly. "Look at you: the perfect male specimen. I'll bet you never gained an excess pound in your life."

"No, but then I work at it every day. If I sat around reading the paper every morning and noshing on Danish pastry instead of jogging five miles, rain, snow or sleet, then maybe I'd have a weight problem, too."

She looked away from his clear eyes, feeling ashamed of her pettiness. Pushing away from the wall, she said, "I think I'll shower. That's all for today, isn't it? You don't have any more torture planned for me, do you?"

"No torture," Kyle said, "but I did want to ask you a favor."

"A favor?" She turned and stared at him. "What kind of favor?"

"I need a date tonight."

"Well, *I* sure don't know anyone you can ask out," she snapped, turning to go. "My God, Kyle, I'm your client not your dating service."

"I meant a date with you."

That stopped her. She stood suspended between disbelief and elation, then slowly turned to face him. "What did you say?"

"You heard me," he said, grinning as he turned to go. "I'll pick you up at seven-thirty."

"Kyle!"

"I won't take no for an answer, Delta. See you then." With that he slammed the door, leaving her staring at it, dumbfounded.

She raced to the door, flung it open and shouted at him, "But I don't know where we're going!"

"Dancing," he shouted back. "Wear your prettiest dress."

Five minutes later Delta stood and glared at her closet. Her prettiest dress. Harrumph. She didn't have a pretty dress she fit into. She was of the "don't throw it out, you'll fit into it again someday" school. Problem was, that day never seemed to come, or as soon as it did, it left again the very next day.

Sighing, Delta slumped onto her bed and contemplated her fate. She had an old tent-shaped dress she could wear, or she could go out and buy something. She hemmed and hawed for five minutes, then grabbed her pocketbook and sprinted downstairs. She'd buy something, by jiminy. She wasn't going out on her first date in almost a year looking like Abdullah the camel herder!

When she opened the door to Kyle at seven-thirty, Delta was wearing a hunter-green silk shirtwaist dress with a plunging neckline and a slit up the front of the skirt. She blinked at Kyle and clutched at the door to keep from melting. He wore a navy linen blazer and white linen slacks and looked wonderful with that dark blond hair falling over his forehead and a warm, appreciative gleam in his eyes.

"Hello," he said, his voice low and sounding strangely intimate.

"Hi," she said, feeling something warm and exciting, yet slightly apprehensive, rise inside her.

"You look terrific," he said, taking her hand and tucking it into the crook of his elbow.

She shivered at his touch, but remembered to make a joke. "Sure," she said sarcastically, "I could become a model for Plus Size clothing when my publisher breaks my contract because I laid an egg on Bill Morton's show."

"You're not going to lay any eggs," he said, leading her toward his car. "You'll do great."

"They say the camera adds ten pounds, Kyle," she said nervously. "Maybe we should shoot for thirty pounds instead of twenty."

"There's no way on earth you'll lose thirty pounds in three weeks, Delta, so forget it. Anyway, all you have to do is wear that dress and everyone will run out to buy your book so they can look like you."

That was going too far. She withdrew her hand from his elbow and fixed him with a cool, speculative gaze. "This is how you do it, isn't it, Kyle? You sweet-talk women into losing weight. You work on their egos."

"Is that what you think I'm doing?"

"You got it," she said airily. "You make a woman feel special and beautiful, and that gets her to feel better about herself, and then she loses weight." She stared at him thoughtfully. "Tell me, though, what happens when you step out of her life, Kyle? Does she keep the weight off, or does she gain it right back because she's so hurt?"

"You really don't think much of me, do you?" he asked, meeting her gaze squarely.

She shrugged. "I can't say I approve of your methods. I'd prefer to keep it strictly business between us. As a matter of fact," she said, turning back toward the house, "I don't think this date tonight's a very good idea."

"Well, you want to know what I think?" Kyle taunted softly. "I think you're chickenhearted. I think you're scared to death to get involved with a man, and when one shows any interest in you whatsoever, you retreat into the kitchen and pig out to make sure he won't find you appealing any longer."

She turned and stared at him with blazing green eyes. "You're full of it."

"Am I? Prove it. Go dancing with me tonight."

She swayed between two poles, unsure whether to tell him to buzz off or take him up on his challenge. Finally she lifted her chin and smiled coolly. "Okay."

"Good," he said, nodding. "That's more like it."

"Just don't try any more sweet talk, Kyle. It makes me nauseated."

"Don't you try any more tough talk," he countered. "It's unbecoming."

"Are you trying to tell me how to act?" she demanded hotly.

"Why not? You just told me how to."

She glared at him, then shouldered past him, opened the car door and threw herself inside. "Well?" she asked irritably. "Are you coming, or are you going to stand out there and gawk at me all night?"

He sighed, shook his head and strolled peaceably around the front of the car, tossing his car keys into the air and catching them while whistling through his teeth. "You're a handful all right," he said when he got into the car.

"Come off it, Kyle," she said sourly, slumping into the seat and folding her arms tightly. "I'm about five handfuls—four more than absolutely necessary."

Instead of answering her, he just smiled lazily and began to chuckle. "You're really funny, Delta," he said, starting the engine. "I can see how you wrote comedy."

She didn't respond. She just turned her head and stared miserably out the car window. She was ruining everything but she couldn't help it. At times she felt as if there were a little demon inside her, punishing her, wreaking havoc on everything she touched. She sniffed back a tear, propped her elbow on the car door and stared dolefully at the passing countryside. If only she looked like Sheila. Everything would be all right then.

* * *

Somehow Kyle had found one of the few places on the Cape that didn't feature loud rock music. A jazz combo played old Billie Holiday, George Gershwin and Cole Porter tunes, and Kyle wouldn't take no for an answer. Taking her by the hand, he led her onto the small dance floor, then took her into his arms.

It was like being swept out to sea, she decided, her heart thumping painfully. His arms were warm around her, and very strong. Somehow they made her feel frail—less heavy, more feminine. He held her close and barely moved around the dance floor, just shuffled his feet. Holding her hand close to his heart, he kept his head close to hers so that she felt dizzy from his nearness and the musky odor of his after-shave.

"Um...have you lived on the Cape long?" she asked, struggling to push him back and put some distance between them.

"Ten years," he said, pulling her close again and burying his head in her hair near her ear.

She shivered at the way his breath seemed to caress her ear, and shoved him back again. "Uh...where were you born?"

"California," he said, pulling her into his embrace once more. "Now stop asking questions and just dance."

His low voice brooked no argument. She relapsed into silence, feeling a warm spiral of desire begin to curl and uncurl in her stomach. For long periods of time she was effectively able to control her libido, but once every few years she met a man who set her pulse to pounding, and that's exactly what Kyle Frederick was doing now. She took a shaky breath and tried to worm out of his embrace, but he growled at her affectionately and only held her closer.

"Stop trying to get away from me," he said lazily. "I'm stronger than you are."

"I'm not trying to get away," she said innocently. "I just want to talk to you, that's all."

"Sure," he said, grinning, "and the sky's purple and clouds are orange."

That shut her up for a few minutes, which allowed Kyle to take strategic advantage of her by humming in her ear while nuzzling the soft skin behind the lobe with his nose. "You smell so good, Delta," he murmured.

"So do you," she breathed dreamily, then could have bitten her tongue.

He lifted his head and peered down into her face. "Do you feel the magic, too?"

She stared into his eyes, transfixed. "The magic?" she asked softly.

"Yeah," he sighed. "The music, the place ... us ..."

"Uh ..." She almost choked. "Us?"

"You and me. We're good together, Delta."

She simply stared. "We are?"

"Mmm," he said, resting his head against hers again and tightening his arms around her. "Can't you feel it? There's electricity between us. It doesn't happen all the time, Delta. It's precious."

She bent her head back and stared up into his face, her eyes solemn. "Why are you saying these things?" she asked, sounding oddly lost and frightened. "You don't have to say them, Kyle. We can just dance. That's enough."

"Not for me, it isn't," he said, his eyes roaming her face. "When I meet a woman who makes me feel the way you do, I like to tell her how I feel."

She swallowed painfully. "Oh," she said in a small voice, then let him draw her into his warm embrace again, her eyes wide, her body suddenly trembling.

"You're so soft, Delta," he said in that low, hypnotic voice. "So womanly. In a way, it's almost a shame you have to lose that weight."

Astounded, she snapped her head back and stared at him. "What?"

He grinned at the expression on her face. "You heard me. I've dated my fair share of women in the past ten years, and all of them have been in really terrific shape. They're lean and mean and muscled, but none of them has made me feel the way I do with you."

She waited for him to go on, but when he didn't, she prodded him. "Which is?"

"Masculine. Protective." He chuckled. *"Aroused,"* he said with a grin.

Her cheeks blossomed with color, and for the first time in years she couldn't think of a humorous comeback. She was saved from having to make a response when the music ended and the band took a break.

At the table Delta fussed in her pocketbook, pretending to search for a tissue. Across from her Kyle watched with amused eyes. "You really are sweet, you know that?" he asked softly.

"Sweet?" she said, raising her head and staring at him. *"Me?"* She couldn't help it; she began to laugh—loudly. "Sweet?" Her laughter rippled up and down the scale, and she shook her head, feeling suddenly on more stable ground. "This is Delta Daniels you're talking to," she said ironically, "the snidest woman in town. My idol is Dorothy Parker. Know what she said when they announced Calvin Coolidge had died?" Kyle shook his head, and she supplied the answer: "How can they tell?"

Kyle grinned, and she grinned back, feeling more comfortable. Humor had always been her sole ally. It was the one thing she could depend on to get her through sticky situations. "When she died, she was cremated. Her epitaph was 'Pardon my dust.'"

Kyle's eyes were warm, his smile magnetic. Delta relaxed and put her elbows on the table, folding her hands and resting her chin on them. "You really think I'm funny?" He nodded. She smiled reflectively. "When I was younger, I wanted to do stand-up comedy. I even did a few comedy clubs in Chicago and New York, but I bombed."

"You should have stuck with it," he said.

She shook her head. "I really don't have the chemistry with a roomful of people. I do better writing for someone else."

"So why'd you stop?"

"The diet books caught on, and I was suddenly making more money writing them." She sighed. "Sometimes I get the urge to do a script for a sitcom though."

"Have you ever done one?"

She shook her head, wrinkling her nose. "Too scared."

"But writing an entire book doesn't scare you?"

"I know diets," she said dryly. "For me, writing a diet book is as easy as falling off a horse."

"I'll have to go out tomorrow and buy your latest book, the one that's number one on the hit parade."

"You don't have to do that," she said softly, pleased by his offer. "Heck, I've got some extra author's copies. I'll give you one."

He shook his head. "I'll buy it. But you'll have to autograph it for me."

She smiled. "You got a deal." She sipped her drink and noticed that the band members had returned. They launched into a drowsy Cole Porter tune, and Kyle stood up and held out his hand.

"Come on," he said. "I want to hold you again."

"I thought it was called dancing," she said wryly.

"That's a euphemism for what it's all about," he said with a lopsided grin.

She floated into his arms, her eyes closed, not about to protest. She was more comfortable with him now and decided it wouldn't hurt to enjoy his nearness for tonight. Tomorrow was soon enough to get back to business. When he nuzzled the skin beneath her ear again, she felt her stomach spin and swirl in a dance of its own.

"God, you feel so good," he growled into her ear. "So warm and curvaceous. Instead of holding bones, I'm holding woman. You don't know what this is doing to me."

She should have reared back and slugged him, but instead she smiled drowsily and put her arms around his neck. "Hush," she murmured. "You're ruining the music."

"Like hell," he said, locking his arms around her. "I'm setting the mood."

She sighed wistfully. "Mmm," she admitted, eyes still closed, a beatific smile curving her lips. "You have a point there."

Kyle groaned and ran his hands up and down her back, then let them rest on her hips. "You're driving me crazy, Delta," he finally said. "We're going to have to either leave or sit down."

She opened her eyes and studied him quizzically. "Are you serious?"

"Absolutely."

She narrowed her eyes. His eyes *were* darker than usual, his pupils enlarged, his face looking slightly strained. There was a kind of animal look about him that made her shiver with expectation. Then she shook her head, her eyes cynical. "Uh-uh, I'm not buying. It's a neat trick, Frederick, but it won't work."

"What trick is that?"

"Trying to raise my self-esteem. I know all the theories on weight gain, you know. I haven't written eight diet books for nothing."

"You really can't believe I'm attracted to you, can you?" he asked, shaking his head at her.

"That's right, I can't. Look at me, Frederick. I'm unpleasantly plump. You yourself admit I have to lose weight."

"Come off it, Delta," he said tiredly. "I agree you should lose weight, but—" He frowned. "I can't explain it. All I know is, I'm *very* attracted. And if we weren't in such a public place, I'd prove it to you."

She gave him a sideways glance that said she didn't believe him, then walked off the dance floor. He was right behind her. "You going somewhere special?" he asked when he caught up with her.

"Yes," she said, smiling sweetly. "Home."

"I suppose this means you expect me to drive you."

"It crossed my mind."

He fished in his pockets, drew out some bills and threw them on the table. Then he took her arm. "Actually, this falls right in with my plans."

"Oh, does it?"

"Yup," he said, sounding self-satisfied and cocky, "it does."

"And just what do your plans include?"

"A stop at a moonlit beach on the way home."

She glanced at him, saw the assurance on his face and knew she was in for it. If Kyle Frederick ever really kissed her, she would gain weight so fast it would make his head swim. He would have her doing five-mile runs, and she in turn would sneak into town and devour gallons of ice cream and dozens of cakes. With all that pushing and pulling, it wouldn't be pleasant.

"No way, Kyle," she said, feigning assurance of her own. "I'm in training. When we get in that car, I expect it not to stop until I'm home. And then I'm leaving you in my dust and making tracks for bed. Alone."

"Buckle your seat belt, Delta," he said matter-of-factly as he started the engine.

"Why? Are we in for a wild ride?"

He glanced at her, his eyes narrowed, his gaze speculative. "We may be at that," he said softly. "We just may be at that...."

Delta snorted softly and turned her head to gaze out the window, hoping her confident facade would convince him. Unfortunately she certainly hadn't convinced herself.

The thing of it was, she wanted to believe he wanted her, but she was afraid to. Some small, nasty, negative voice far back in her unconscious seemed always to be shouting messages at her: *Don't trust anyone. No one could ever love you. Forget about a future with a man. Who would want to be involved with someone like you?*

Struggling against those negative messages had always been too much for her. She'd never been able to banish them completely and had always fallen back into the self-defeating pattern of overeating to compensate for lack of involvement with a man. But there was something inside her, some hopeful part that refused to give up, that kept raising its little head and whispering to her, telling her to take a chance and see what happened when she allowed herself to believe.

She turned her head quietly and looked at Kyle, studying him, trying to figure out what he really wanted from her. Could he really be attracted to her? She suddenly remembered that silly game she'd played as a child—the one with the daisies. You picked a daisy and plucked the petals off one by one, keeping count as you went, shifting between two alternatives: He loves me, he loves me not. Whichever one you ended on was the truth.

She sighed and turned sad eyes out the window. Always, always in her life, she'd ended on "he loves me not." Believing in herself, believing she was lovable, seemed the most impossible task on earth. It required faith, and trust, and hope, and she was woefully lacking in all three.

It was like standing on a precipice, she mused. She stood on the edge, staring down into the dark abyss, and fear rose up and paralyzed her until she couldn't move—she couldn't go backward and couldn't make that leap of faith forward. So she tottered in limbo, each year growing more afraid to go forward, yet paradoxically less able to retreat.

She closed her eyes and rested her head against the car seat. It was no use. She was going to give up. She would resign herself to a life alone, a life of diet books and weight swings, to the comforts of big fat hot fudge sundaes and ice-cream cones and pizza and doughnuts.

Suddenly the car slowed and she felt it lurch off the road. She sat up and looked around. "Are we home already?"

"Hardly," Kyle said. "We're at the beach."

She looked at him, her mouth set in a firm line. "I told you I wanted to go home."

"I know what you said, Delta," he responded, "but I wanted to come here."

"And I suppose you always put your own desires first?"

"When they're really your desires, too, yes."

"What the heck do you mean by that?" she asked irritably.

The car rolled to a stop and Kyle cut the engine. The sudden quiet was broken by the sound of surf rolling in, by the hiss of spray against sand and the lapping of water against the rock jetties. Moonlight speckled a frosted path across the ocean, dancing and glittering on the water, seeming to lead directly from the sky to their car.

Kyle turned in the seat and fixed his eyes on Delta. "I mean, Delta," he said quietly, "that you want to kiss me as much as I want to kiss you."

She sat frozen, hypnotized by uncertainty. Slowly Kyle reached out and brushed his fingers softly against the pale skin of her cheek. She took an unsteady breath and tried to turn away, but he fastened his hand on her chin and turned her face resolutely toward his.

"Delta," he murmured, his breath warm on her lips. "Kiss me."

She ran. She opened the car door and bolted so fast she was just a blur in the night. The breeze caught her hair, and the scent of salt spray assaulted her senses so that when she finally stopped running she was at the edge of the water, her lungs filled with the briny odor of ocean, her heart pounding painfully.

Somewhere along the way she'd kicked off her heels and now stood on the damp edge of the sea, her arms crossed tightly over her breasts, her shoulders hunched against any possible invasion.

"You can run, Delta," Kyle said softly from just behind her, "but you can't hide forever."

She lifted her chin and stared stonily at the water. "Leave me alone, Kyle Frederick. You're a fitness trainer, not a therapist."

"I'm a man, first and foremost, and you're a woman. This has nothing to do with therapy."

She shivered and rubbed her arms distractedly, her eyes troubled as she continued to stare out to sea. "Don't do this, Kyle," she said quietly. "Please. Let's just be friends, okay? It'll be so much simpler if that's all we are."

"But life isn't simple, Delta. Life's complex. That's what makes it so beautiful." He reached down and picked up a shell and held it out to her. "See?" He indicated the whorls that patterned its surface, pointed out the intricate convolutions and indentions. "Once, not very long ago, there was a life in this shell, Delta. A simple life in a simple shell, yet it's all part of a greater world, so complex and mysterious we have no idea what it's all about."

He pressed the shell into her hand. "We're all part of that world, Delta. We can't disengage from it, can't set ourselves apart. If we do, we die inside. We need each other, Delta. It's a law of nature."

She stared down at the shell, feeling tears prick at her eyes. Somehow that shell seemed to be the most beautiful, most wonderful object she had ever held. But she couldn't turn to Kyle, couldn't trust herself or him, couldn't allow herself to become involved. She traced the surface of the shell with her fingers, feeling the grains of sand that encrusted it, along with the cool dampness from the sea. A strange sadness welled up within her, as if she were listening to angels weeping over some terrible loss.

Unable to bear it, she turned and hurried toward the car, the shell pressed tightly in her hand, tears threatening to spill over. She was sitting quietly in the car, clutching the shell, when Kyle returned.

"I'm sorry, Delta," he said. "I had no right to force you like this."

She shook her head. "It doesn't matter."

"I'll take you home."

She merely nodded. There was nothing to say, nothing in the world.

Five

"Get a move on, Delta." Kyle's command shattered the early-morning air. Delta turned rebellious eyes toward him and muttered an oath under her breath. He was worse than a slave driver; he was a fiend, delighting in punishing her. Her body was one entire ache. Her muscles screamed out for relief, but none was forthcoming. She sniffed to herself as she jogged down the winding road that skirted Cape Cod Bay. He was just getting back at her for not kissing him last Saturday night. For the past five days he'd been like this. His male ego was wounded, but he was being especially cruel this morning.

"You're not jogging, Delta," Kyle barked. "You're shuffling. Get the lead out. Pick up those feet and breathe in deeply. Get some spring into your step."

Delta gritted her teeth but refused to bark back. That's probably what he wanted—to goad her into a fight. Instead, she picked up the pace of her jog and lifted her face to the cool morning breeze. The fog had burned off, leaving a golden sun glowing in the bright blue sky. The water in the bay glittered and sparkled, gulls screeched and the ocean lapped unendingly onto the shore, its sibilant murmur a constant undertone beneath the early morning silence.

The only other sounds were the steady beat of her and Kyle's jogging feet and the labored breathing in her tortured lungs. Kyle was disgustingly in shape—he wouldn't be out of breath after running a marathon, she suspected.

"You're looking good, Delta," Kyle said.

She jumped in surprise at the way he'd glided up beside her, and cast him an incredulous look. "Who? Me? Old Flabby Thighs herself?"

"Your legs are already toning up, whether you know it or not. You're looking really good."

"Don't try to get on my good side, Frederick," she said, proud that she could talk and jog at the same time. A few days ago, she couldn't.

"I didn't know you had a good side," Kyle said dryly.

She shot him an almost amused look. "I don't. If you remember that, you'll do all right with me."

"Why would I even try?" Kyle countered. "Last Saturday night you shot me down pretty effectively."

Delta frowned to herself, feeling an immediate sense of contrition. She *had* been pretty mean to Kyle, but how could she admit it without sounding as if she were encouraging his advances? She coasted to a stop and stood puffing, trying to gather courage to broach the subject.

"You okay?" Kyle asked, coming to a stop next to her.

She hesitated, then shook her head. "No, I'm not okay. I'm sorry about how I treated you Saturday. I know you were only trying to be kind, to get me to think better of myself, but I just can't handle that, Kyle. I'd like for us to be friends. Let's not play games with each other, okay?"

"Who's playing games?" he asked, taking her by the arm and pulling her along at a fast walk.

"Oh, Kyle, come off it," she said exasperatedly. "Look at me! I'm twenty pounds overweight and look like Flipper, the daughter of Flubber. I jiggle when I walk, and positively *undulate* when I jog. We're talking major numbers on the Richter scale. I'll bet every time I jog in the morning, somewhere some seismologist is scratching his head in amazement, trying to figure out where the damned earthquake on Cape Cod is coming from.''

Kyle looked as if he were trying to keep from laughing, then he began to chuckle. ''Dammit, Delta,'' he said finally, laughter rumbling in his chest, ''you really are funny.''

She grinned at him and escalated into a jog. ''Come on, Frederick,'' she barked in perfect imitation of him, ''let's get cracking. Pick up those feet. Breathe deeply. Run, buster, run.''

They were laughing when they reached her home, both convulsed by the stories she related about Jerry Connors, the television comedian she had written for. As she giggled, Delta fell to the ground and held her stomach, which ached from the combination of laughter and hard exercise. Kyle leaned against the house and gave way to merriment.

''And *then*,'' Delta said between gasps, ''he turns to me and says, 'Who sez? You and what damn army?' ''

Kyle slid down the house until he was on the ground, his back against the house, tears of laughter streaming down his face, his shoulders shaking even harder. ''Stop!'' he gasped. ''Stop it, Delta, my stomach hurts.''

''So does mine,'' she wailed, rolling into a ball and clutching at her midriff, then bursting out into fresh gales. ''He's such a jerk, Kyle. I mean, on television he's funny and all, but in person? The guy's a loser. I used to write the best damn material, and sometimes he wouldn't get it.''

Kyle's laughter died out gradually until he was just sitting with his back against the house, smiling at Delta. ''It must have been fun writing material for all those guys.''

She lay back and stared dreamily up at the sky. ''Yeah,'' she said wistfully. ''Sometimes I miss it.''

''So go back to it, Delta.''

She shook her head. ''Nah, I'm too old for that life, Kyle, and anyway, we're talking major stress—writing for television. They fire people the way Attila the Hun burned villages. There's no such thing as job security. Everything's the ratings. If the Nielsens go down a fraction of a point, you can kiss the paycheck goodbye and start pounding the pavement.''

''But it can't be much easier writing books.''

She grinned wryly. ''You got a point there. You never know if you'll get another contract.'' She smiled reflectively. ''But I'm my own boss. I work when I want to, and the royalty checks are nice.''

''Sounds like a good life.''

Delta turned questioning eyes to him. ''What about you? Do you like what you're doing?''

''Love it. I don't know anything else, Delta. My entire life's been sports and fitness.'' His face clouded. ''Every once in a while, though, I get a little scared. I wonder what I'd do if I ever got hurt, say in an accident or something, and couldn't do what I've always done. I mean, what would happen to me? Sometimes I think I should find some new interests, or go back to school and get some kind of useful degree.''

Delta lay stretched out on the ground, staring at Kyle. She was enormously touched, and the sweet warmth that invaded her suddenly filled her soul with kinship and compassion. ''Don't you have any other interests besides fitness, Kyle?''

He shrugged. ''I fish a little, and play a little golf, and sail.'' He frowned again. ''But see? They're all active, physical things. I need something for my mind, something stimulating.''

Delta gnawed on that for a while, frowning, then said, ''How about books? Do you read at all?''

Kyle grinned. ''Yeah—about sports. I've read every major league ballplayer's autobiography, every golfer's tips for successful play, every story about sailing around the Cape of Good Hope.''

''Mmm,'' Delta said, ''you *do* have a problem.'' She cocked her head inquiringly. ''What about concerts, plays, movies?''

He shrugged. "I don't have time for them. Well, I guess I have time, but I've just never bothered to get involved in anything like that."

Delta bit the corner of her mouth, pondering a major suggestion. She needed a way to make up for treating him so rudely last Saturday. Perhaps if she just offered to be his friend, he would let up on those ridiculous passes he'd made that night. "Look," she said tentatively, "I'd be willing to go with you to a few plays or concerts—you know, just so you could find out if you like them or not."

"You would?" Kyle asked, sounding absurdly happy.

Delta's face softened with a smile. "Sure," she said gently. "Hey, we're going to be friends, aren't we?"

Suddenly he was unreadable. "Yeah," he said slowly. "I guess we are. That'd be great, Delta. When would you be willing to start?"

"Oh..." She shrugged. "Soon. I'll check the paper and see what's going on tonight, then we can decide what we'd like to do."

"That'd be great, Delta," Kyle said, smiling. "I really appreciate your interest."

She stood up and dusted off the seat of her pants, waving away his words. "Think nothing of it," she said, walking tiredly toward the house. "Right now, all I want is a plate of flapjacks with maple syrup oozing off them with oodles of butter, and bacon, sausage, great big mugs of coffee and—"

"Hot water and lemon," Kyle interrupted dryly.

She paused at the door, her shoulders slumping. "Okay," she said dispiritedly, "hot water and lemon it'll be."

In the kitchen Delta leaned against the counter and sipped her glass of hot water and lemon while she paged through the paper, looking for likely entertainment. She ran down the listing of activities for that night. There was a concert at Cape Cod Community College, a production of the Provincetown Theater Company, a string quartet playing in Falmouth, a poetry reading at a Falmouth bookstore, another concert, square dancing, a lecture on marsh birds, and dozens of other events. She'd be happy to go to any of them, but what about Kyle?

"Find anything?" Kyle asked from behind her.

She jumped, then managed to shrug. "There's lots of stuff going on. I'm just not sure what you'd enjoy."

"Here, let me take a look." He took the paper from her and skimmed the page, then pointed to an ad. "This. I'll pick you up at eight-thirty tonight." With that, he turned and strode toward the door. "Remember not to do your weight training today, Delta. Your muscles need a day to recuperate. We'll work out on the weights again tomorrow."

"Are you leaving?" she asked, suddenly feeling disappointed.

"Yeah." He smiled from the door. "But I'll see you tonight. Wear something pretty."

She watched him disappear through the door, then turned and stared down at the ad he'd pointed to. "Tonight," it read, "Bill Carver at the piano with the Carver Quintet. Dancing nine to one."

She stood and stared down at the ad, steam rising from her like heat from an August sidewalk. Dammit, he'd tricked her! Her mouth thinned into a narrow, determined line. Well, Kyle Frederick was in for a surprise. She wasn't about to let him try his seduction act again. She wasn't interested, and tonight she planned to make that abundantly clear.

That night, when Delta opened the door, Kyle stared at her in disbelief. "I'm sorry," he said at last. "I guess you're not ready yet."

She shook her head. "I'm ready," she said, smiling brightly.

He let his gaze travel up and down her body, taking in the worn denim overalls she wore over a tank top. One overall knee was ripped, and when she turned to get her pocketbook, he saw there was a saucy hole on her right thigh. Squinting, he could just make out the pale pink of her skin.

He felt a jolt of electricity travel through his midsection, and his fingers begin to itch with desire.

Then she turned back, and his gaze rose to her full breasts, which swelled softly beneath her tank top and overall bib. He felt a stirring in his loins at the thought of how they would feel in his hands—heavy and sweet-smelling, with nipples like dusky rosebuds.

He bit back a low groan of agonized pleasure and forced himself to raise his gaze to her face. She was looking triumphant and proud, as if she'd pulled off some feat meant solely to antagonize him. She didn't know it but her ploy of dressing sloppily to turn him off had backfired. He loved the way her body curved softly beneath those ridiculous overalls, loved the lush curve of her breasts, the hint of flesh exposed through that naughty hole. Still, it wouldn't do to let her know that. He fought to assume a disappointed expression.

"Um, I thought we'd go dancing, Delta."

"So?" She shrugged. "Can't I dance in overalls?"

He shrugged and gnawed on the corner of his mouth. "Well, there might be a dress code."

"If there's a dress code, we'll just have to leave and find someplace where there isn't one."

He heaved a sigh and shrugged again. "Well, if that's what you want to wear...."

"It is," she said shortly. Then she swung her pocketbook over her shoulder and sailed past him, head held high, chin up.

He grinned to himself, letting his gaze travel down her lush body, enjoying the way her hips swung saucily.

At the car she turned and spied his expression, and he had to work fast to wipe it off and assume a noncommittal look. She narrowed her eyes as he approached her.

"Are you angry about the way I'm dressed?" she asked, looking suspicious.

"Angry? Why no. I'm just a little disappointed, that's all." He slyly gauged the impact of his words. "I mean, when a man takes a woman out dancing, he likes her to dress up a little.''

She shrugged complacently. "But I'm not just any woman," she said. "And we're not going out on a date. We're just getting you out to sample the joys of nonathletic events."

He cleared his throat and kept his gaze averted as he got into the car and started the engine. If he had his way—which he firmly intended to do before the night was over—their little excursion would turn into a decidedly athletic event!

Something wasn't right. Delta frowned to herself, then shrugged away her doubts. Kyle was just being a gentleman about her clothes. He couldn't actually *like* the way she'd dressed. She had done it purposely to embarrass him. What man wanted to be seen in public with a tubby tuna dressed in dumpy overalls? But for some strange reason, Kyle was smiling and attentive and seemingly not annoyed by the spectacle she must have presented on the dance floor of one of Cape Cod's nicest cocktail lounges.

There had been a touchy moment at the door when the maître d', or whatever he was, had looked askance at her attire, then shrugged and let her and Kyle in. But other than that no one seemed to pay any particular attention to her, and here she was cradled in Kyle's arms on the dance floor, feeling soft, frail, feminine and decidedly special.

She stopped thinking and gave herself up to the pleasure of being held in his arms. She'd danced with dozens of men, but she'd never been held quite so gently, so tenderly, as if she were some rare and precious treasure. Her body melted into his, and they moved together easily, as if they had been dancing with each other forever. Warmth seemed to shimmer inside her, burning like a low pilot flame, urging her to press her body into his, to feel his leg brushing hers, her breasts crushed against his powerful chest....

She snapped out of her reverie and cleared her throat, pushing away and smiling brightly. "So!" she said gaily. "Nice place, huh?"

His eyes seemed to bore into hers. He didn't smile, didn't respond at all, just stared into her eyes, his own looking dark and almost smoky, which was strange, because she knew they were blue. She felt her stomach curl up inside her like a kitten on a warm hearth, felt her heart begin to beat faster, felt her mouth go dry, her breathing quicken. She turned her head in an effort to break the magnetic pull, but he only fastened a gentle hand on her chin and forced her to look back at him.

"Don't look away from me, Delta," he said softly.

She swallowed painfully and met his gaze, feeling strange quiverings begin deep inside her.

"You dressed this way on purpose, didn't you?" he asked.

"On purpose?" she squeaked.

He nodded slowly, his eyes holding hers. "To try to stymie me. To keep me from making another pass at you."

She looked everywhere but at him. "I don't know what you mean. I *like* overalls. They're comfortable, and I feel more natural in them, and—"

"Oh, stop pretending, Delta," Kyle said tiredly. "Your silly games are immature."

His harsh words stung her, forcing her to look back at him, her eyes flashing. "I can't be that immature," she snapped, "since you're interested enough to pursue me."

A slow smile grew on his face. "That's right. I am interested. What are you going to do about it?"

She glanced idly around at the couples on the dance floor. "Nothing," she said finally, managing to sound bored, her eyes at last meeting his. "I've only got to put up with your nonsense for two more weeks until I appear on Bill Morton's show."

"You think I'll stop chasing you then?"

She nodded, her lips twisted in a sarcastic grin. "Yes, I do."

"You don't know the first thing about men, do you?" he asked, sliding his hands possessively down her back and resting them on her hips. He pulled her closer so that her abdomen was pressed against him.

She felt warning flares go off, but couldn't pull away, couldn't break eye contact with him. "I know enough," she said, sounding breathless and cursing her body for betraying her.

He shook his head. One corner of his mouth lifted in amusement. "If you knew anything, you'd have let me kiss you last Saturday night. You wouldn't have gone running off like some frightened teenager."

She lifted her head at that, and high color invaded her cheeks. "I'm not entirely innocent," she said coolly. "I've had a few affairs in my time."

He cocked his head inquiringly. "Have you now? With whom? Lily-livered boys who were afraid to show you what a real man wants from a woman?"

She was so angry that she felt herself begin to shake. Her eyes blazed into his, but she refused to be baited. "I don't want to talk about it," she said.

"Of course you don't," he said, chuckling. "You're walking on quicksand, and you know it. You need to get back on dry land, to talk about diets and how fat you think you are, things that make you comfortable. Talking about men and sex and love scares you too much."

"Love!" she crowed. "What would *you* know about love?"

"A hell of a lot more than you, I'll bet."

She burned with rage, tried out a dozen scathing responses, but none seemed scathing enough. Finally she settled on snorting and lifting her chin disdainfully.

"What's the matter, Delta?" he asked lazily. "No comeback?"

"I just prefer not to waste my energy," she said frostily.

He began to chuckle. "You little fraud," he said, sounding almost affectionate, "you're seething inside, you're so angry, but you know I'm right, so you can't say anything."

"Right?" she said, wanting to shout but keeping her voice down to a low hiss. "Ha!"

He pulled her closer and rested his chin against her head. "You're so damned lovable," he said softly. "So sweet and lonely and sad. I just want to hold you, Delta, to protect you."

She stared at the wiry blond hairs visible above the open collar of his shirt. She felt frightened. When he talked like that, she went all soft and fluttery. She felt strange yearnings to be held in just the way he claimed he wanted to hold her.

"Stop fighting me, Delta," he crooned in her ear. "Just relax. Let things happen. Don't worry about tomorrow or next week or next year. Live for today, tonight."

She took a trembling breath and closed her eyes, resting her cheek against his powerful chest. She couldn't fight him, didn't even want to try. His message was too seductive, and she was too needy. She knew that tomorrow he would change his tune—or next week, or the week after—but that suddenly didn't matter anymore. The only thing that mattered was his strong arms, and the sustenance he offered her.

"Okay," she breathed, feeling more frightened than she ever had in her life. "I won't fight you anymore, but Kyle—"

"Yes?" His arms were warm around her, gentle, and his lips caressed her temple.

"Don't pretend to feel something you don't," she begged softly. "I've been hurt enough in my life. I don't need to be hurt any more."

He didn't say anything right away, and she was immediately afraid she'd said the wrong thing. She pushed away, looked up into his face and was startled to see compassion there.

"I'm not going to hurt you," he said softly. "I promise you, Delta, I won't ever hurt you."

She immediately remembered Jack Peterson, her first boyfriend, and the promises he'd whispered in the honeysuckle-scented spring nights. "Please, Kyle, don't ever promise anything," she said in a tortured whisper. "Promises never last."

His face was troubled as he pulled her back into the shelter of his arms. "Never?" he asked.

She shook her head, her eyes squeezed shut, her hands clutching at his shirt. "Never."

He ran a gentle hand up and down her back and stared thoughtfully over her head. "Sometimes they do," he finally said.

She didn't answer. What was there to say to such an absurdity? Kyle had just called her immature, when all along he was the child, utterly innocent in the ways of the world. There was no such thing as true devotion. It was all a pack of lies, a snarled web of need and desire and personal gain. No one truly thought of the other person; everyone thought only of himself.

The music ended, and Kyle led her back to their table, then called for the check and escorted her from the cocktail lounge to the car. Once there, he sat staring moodily out at the parking lot, lost in thought. It was as if she weren't even there.

Delta moved uneasily in the seat, uncomfortably aware that she had said something to put a damper on the evening. Miserably she turned her head and looked out the side window. The night was cool and moonlit, scented with the slight tang of ocean air and early spring flowers. She took a shaky breath and looked back at Kyle. She was startled to find him watching her, his face thoughtful, almost abstracted.

"I'm sorry I ruined your night," she said softly. "I seem to have that capacity."

He shook his head, reaching out and taking her hand in his. "I was wrong to bring you dancing again," he said slowly. "I should have chosen a lecture or a concert or a play."

She nodded, feeling her heart tumble from its hopeful perch. "That's okay," she said, forcing a smile. "I know why you felt you needed to date me."

"But I—" He broke off suddenly, then shook his head. "I'd like to be your friend, Delta. And I meant it when I said I'd appreciate your going with me to some social events. Will you still go out with me?''

She relaxed, feeling more comfortable in this easy relationship. ''Sure, I'd be glad to.''

''Good. Tomorrow night let's go to a concert or a play. But let's go out to dinner first—'' He broke off, his gaze flying to hers worriedly. ''Uh-oh. I guess we can't go out to dinner, can we?''

She smiled lopsidedly. ''Well, we *could*, but all your hard work would go down the drain.''

He frowned. ''Look, we could still go out for dinner. You could just order a salad and a glass of water, and I'd eat a regular meal. How about it?''

She shrugged. ''It seems a waste of money to me, but you're the one who wants to go out.''

''Good,'' he said, almost sounding happy. ''I'll make reservations, and I'll pick you up at six.''

She settled into her seat, feeling relief blossom inside her. There'd be no more silly seductions, no more pretense between them. Maybe they'd become friends. Lord knows, she needed all the friends she could get.

Six

———

"Tell me about yourself, Delta," Kyle said the next night at dinner.

Delta smiled. "There's nothing much to tell. I'm originally from Chicago. I've got a half sister—" Delta rolled her eyes comically. "She's incredibly gorgeous. If you saw her, you'd flip." She tilted her head to the side and considered. "I majored in theater in college, I'm a Cancer and my hobbies are cooking and eating and a little gardening—" she grinned "—mostly to pick the vegetables that go into my dinner."

"Tell me about your half sister."

Delta's smile vanished. Suddenly it was as if a cloud had covered the sun. She sat back and sighed tiredly. "Sheila," she said slowly. "I told you—she's absolutely beautiful. That's all you need to know about her. When she was born, the doctors stopped breathing and just stared in awe. She was born beautiful and she's remained beautiful."

"What's she do?"

"Do?" Delta chuckled wryly. "She models occasionally, but mostly she flits from relationship to relationship, appearing nightly on some fantastically wealthy man's arm at the opera or the theater or the best restaurants."

"You sound as if you don't much care for her."

Delta felt a pang go through her. Her jealousy of her half sister always caused her pain. She knew she shouldn't be jealous, but she couldn't help it. Everything had always come easily to Sheila. Nothing had ever come easily to Delta—except gaining weight.

She sipped her water and toyed with a response to Kyle's comment. Finally she shrugged. "She's always been my mother's favorite. She was the daughter of my mother's first husband. My own dad died before I was born, so there's just been my mom and Sheila and me, the unholy trinity." She laughed mirthlessly. "Of course there's generally a new stepfather every couple of years or so. But they never last."

"Doesn't sound like the happiest family in America."

Delta shrugged, tired of the subject. "We got by."

"When did you start gaining weight?"

"In college. I remember the day I went on my first eating binge as if it were just yesterday."

Kyle picked at his appetizer, his eyes shadowed behind his lashes. "Pretty memorable, eh?"

"Memorable is right," Delta said soulfully. "I ate my way through a dozen doughnuts and a six-pack of Snickers bars, then topped it all off with two pizzas, a couple of hamburgers, and a gallon of Nut Chocolate Fudge ice cream."

"Something pretty painful must have triggered it, I guess."

Delta was about to respond, but she stopped herself, looking at Kyle suspiciously. She shrugged instead, refusing to open up. "I can't remember what started it, actually."

"No?"

She stared into his eyes, daring him to doubt her word. "No," she said clearly, her tone brooking no argument.

He shrugged. "That seems odd. You remember exactly what you ate, but you can't remember why."

"That's right," she said coolly. "I can't."

"Were you away at school at the time?"

"No, I was home," she responded automatically, then wished she hadn't.

"I see," he said, then sat back and sighed contentedly.

Delta felt her mouth water as she stared longingly at his empty plate.

Kyle shook his head sorrowfully. "I'm sorry, Delta, honey. It's mean of me to eat in front of you like this."

She smiled, warmed by his endearment. "That's okay, Kyle. Life goes on for others, even when all joy has ended for me."

"All joy?" he asked quizzically. "Doesn't my company mean anything?"

She laughed away his question. "You know what I mean. Joy equals food to me. It's the equation I live by."

"You need to change that equation, Delta."

She let out a long sigh and nodded. "Yeah, I know."

"You don't appear too happy about that."

She rubbed at an invisible spot on the linen tablecloth. "I guess I'm like a junkie," she said, "or an alcoholic. Food's my drug and my drink."

"Even junkies and alcoholics can be cured, Delta," Kyle said gently.

The tenderness in his voice reached into her, making her feel special. She smiled at him. "Thank you for helping me, Kyle. I feel very fortunate that you care so much."

"I'm glad you realize I *do* care," he answered. "It's not just another job for me, you know."

"Why?"

He considered her question, then shrugged. "I find you attractive, Delta, not only physically but..." He searched for the right words. "Emotionally, I guess is what I mean. Something in you reaches out to me and I respond." He lifted his broad shoulders helplessly and let them fall. "I can't explain it. I just care."

For the first time she began to realize he might be telling the truth. Troubled by this realization and the knowledge that she'd been turning him away, she frowned thoughtfully. "Not too many people have cared about me in my life," she said slowly.

"It was their loss then," he said gently.

She lifted her eyes and stared into his, seeing tenderness and warmth and something else, something that made her want to get up and run away. She felt anxiety dart through her, like a mouse scampering across a kitchen floor, and suddenly she had to make a joke, had to defuse this strange situation.

She crossed her eyes at him and made a funny face. "Gee," she said, imitating Goofy's voice, "do you really think so, Kyle? Guffaw. Guffaw. Guffaw."

At first he didn't smile. When he did, his expression was slow, almost tired but accepting of her all the same. "You don't need to always joke with me, Delta," he said finally. "You can be serious once in a while, you know."

"That's just the trouble," she said sadly. "I can't be serious, Kyle. I never could."

"We'll see about that," he said softly. "Maybe we can work on that while we take off those excess pounds."

"A whole make-over, eh?" she asked cheerfully.

"Yeah," he said, nodding. "An entirely new woman."

She looked away, not sure of how to react, but something hopeful rose inside her, that small voice that was usually drowned out by negativism. It told her not to let this guy get away—it might be the only chance she ever got.

She turned her head and looked back at him thoughtfully, watching as he smiled at the waitress who deposited a plate of swordfish and broccoli in front of him. What a strange man he was. A very strange man indeed.

They ended up going for a walk on the beach in Hyannis. The last remnants of red stained the western sky, the moon dappled the water with frosted silver and the ocean lulled them with its ceaseless murmur. She kept her distance, still worried he might try to kiss her, but she realized after a few minutes that she needn't be concerned at all. He was almost ignoring her, picking up rocks and skipping them on the ocean, or flinging them as far as he could and listening for the splash in the darkness.

Though she should have been happy he was leaving her alone, she was disappointed. Some insane demon inside her wished he was pouncing on her, making her feel desirable. Finally she sat down on the rocks of a jetty that jutted into the ocean and watched him pick up rocks one by one and hurl them out to sea.

As she watched, she stopped thinking about herself and tuned him in, and she suddenly realized he was angry or frustrated, or both. Troubled by his mood, she fought with herself, wondering if she should try to talk to him. Finally she decided she had nothing to lose.

"Kyle," she said softly. "What's wrong?"

He didn't answer right away. Finally he hurled the last rock far out into the water and turned to her. "Nothing's wrong. Why?"

"You seem angry."

He put a foot up on the rocks and shoved his hands into his trouser pockets. "Do I?"

Now she wasn't so sure. He was watching her intently, but he didn't look angry. He seemed almost amused, as if he were taunting her. She frowned. What could he possibly be taunting her about? She shook her head. "I guess I was wrong," she said doubtfully.

"I guess you were," he countered, one corner of his mouth lifting in a wry grin.

She stared at him belligerently, then hopped down from the jetty and stalked away, wishing that sand didn't give way underfoot so easily. It made stomping off with dignity difficult.

"Where you going?" Kyle shouted, laughing.

"Home," she snapped over her shoulder, hair blowing about her head in wild disarray.

"You're going in the wrong direction," he yelled.

She kept walking, so angry she could spit. "I'll get there eventually," she yelled back. "The Cape's small. Every road eventually leads home."

She heard Kyle's footsteps come bounding up behind her, heard his chuckle, then his hand was on her arm and he was spinning her around to face him. "Isn't it about time you grew up, Delta?" he asked, his head cocked inquiringly, eyes gleaming devilishly.

"Me?" she asked, laughing disdainfully. "What about you? You're the eternal youth, exercising that gorgeous body of yours so you never grow old."

"Is that what my body is, Delta? Gorgeous?"

She tossed her head and folded her arms, staring out at the water. "Oh..." She harrumphed. "You know what I mean."

"Yeah, I think I do," he said softly, reaching out to run his fingers through her wind-tossed curls.

She tugged her head away, turned on her heel and headed back down the beach from where she'd come. Kyle stood with his hands on his hips, watching her, then he shook his head, grinning, and set out after her.

"You angry or something, Delta?" he asked when he caught up with her.

"No," she snapped.

"Sure sounds like you are."

"That's how much *you* know."

He sighed mightily and began to whistle tunelessly between his teeth. "Say, want to build sand castles?"

That stopped her in her tracks. She turned and stared at him, then set off again. "No. And look who's the kid in this duo."

"Okay, so I'm a kid. Why don't you want to build sand castles?"

"We don't have a shovel and pail."

"Don't need them. We have hands."

"Fine," she said. "Use your own hands. *I'm* going home."

"Can't," he said.

"Why can't I?"

He dangled his car keys in front of her. "'Cause I have these."

She swiped at them, but he lifted them out of her reach. "Come on, Delta," he said, laughing. "Let's build just one castle."

"Fine," she said, folding her arms and tapping her toe. "Build."

"It's no fun building castles by yourself, Delta. You have to have a partner."

She broke off a low oath and dropped to her knees. "You win," she said, beginning to dig in the sand. "Come on, get digging."

Kyle dropped down next to her and grinned at her. "Feels like we're kids again, doesn't it?"

She fought a smile, but it wavered on her lips. "You're impossible," she said, trying to sound mean.

He let a trail of sand sift through his fingers, then sat back on his heels and inhaled deeply. "Lord, I love it here."

Delta's face softened. She sat back, too, breathing in deeply. "Yeah," she said. "I'm so glad I moved to the Cape. It's everything New York City isn't—clean, peaceful, fragrant."

"Know what I love?" he asked. She shook her head. "The air," he said. "It's got that tangy bite to it, like a crisp apple in the fall. You fill your lungs with it and somehow you feel clean inside."

She smiled dreamily, leaning over to smooth a mound of sand into an approach ramp for the castle. "Yeah," she mused. "And the water, of course. You're never far from the water on the Cape. I'm always peaceful near the water."

"You weren't tonight," Kyle pointed out. "Or last night."

She threw him an exasperated look. "That's because of you."

"You mean you're not peaceful around me?"

"Hardly." She rolled her eyes at him comically. "You make me want to scream."

"Why?"

She smiled, piling sand into a turret. "Because you're obstinate. You force me to starve myself. You make me exercise as if you're some kind of slave driver. You yell at me and hound me and then have the audacity to tell me I'm attractive."

"You are."

She shook her head. "It won't wash, Kyle."

"You ever look in all those mirrors you have hanging around your house?"

She laughed. "All the time."

"What do you see?"

"A fat woman."

"Exactly," he said, sounding triumphant. "That's what you see, but you're not fat. You're slightly plump and you're out of shape. We'll remedy both of those in the next two weeks. It'll be interesting to see what you see in your mirrors then."

She sighed wistfully, sitting back and staring out to sea, watching the way the moon glittered on the water, seeing the frosted lace wash up on the shore, leaving gilded bubbles in its wake. "I would like to keep the weight off this time, Kyle," she said. "Maybe I could start working out at your gym regularly."

"I think that's a great idea, Delta."

She turned to look at him and smiled. "Thanks for putting up with me. I've always been headstrong. As a matter of fact, I've never met a man yet who could handle me."

"Oh?"

She shook her head, remembering the men she'd met and dated and gained weight over. "No. It's funny—I have no willpower when it comes to eating, but I'm generally a very strong woman." She turned and looked at Kyle. "Men don't like strong women, you know."

"They don't?"

"They don't." She laughed harshly. "They want someone who smiles and simpers and bats her eyelashes at them and tells them how big and strong they are."

"That's not what I want in a woman," Kyle said.

"Oh? What do you want, Kyle? Thirty-eight, twenty-four, thirty-six?"

"No. One-forty."

She stared down at the castle that was beginning to materialize out of the sand. "What's that supposed to mean?"

"That's what you weigh, isn't it?"

Slowly she looked up and met his eyes. "Don't try to charm me, Kyle. It won't work."

"I'm not trying to charm you," he said. "I'm serious."

She looked away, suddenly uncomfortable. No matter what they did together, sooner or later everything came back to the subject of "them." "Maybe we'd better go," she said.

"Maybe we shouldn't," he said. "Maybe we should stay and see what happens."

She shrugged, acting unconcerned. "Why, the castle will get built and then the tide will come and sweep it away—that's what'll happen."

"I'm not talking about the castle. I'm talking about us."

She went very still. He was entirely too close. Somehow while they'd been talking he'd maneuvered himself closer so that his arm just brushed hers. She could almost feel his breath on her cheek, could just detect the aroma of his after-shave mingling with the spicy tang of salt air.

She felt apprehension and excitement mount inside her, felt a delicious sense of imminent physical contact. Electricity seemed to crackle in the air. The world fell away, leaving only Kyle. He reached out, brushed his fingers against her cheek, then leaned forward and lazily kissed her earlobe.

She exhaled softly, beginning to quiver with excitement. Her eyelids drifted down. Kyle wrapped his arms around her, pulling her into his embrace. Neither of them said a word when he bent and nibbled the soft skin of her neck, then kissed her ear again, gently, like a breeze kissing the clouds.

It was his gentleness that undid her. She couldn't resist his tenderness, the sweetness that his lips and arms promised.

She lifted her face, her eyes still closed, her expression rapt, and let his lips travel over it, dropping petal-soft kisses on her cheeks, her forehead, her eyelids, her nose, then down her neck and into the hollow of her throat.

He bent her backward in his strong arms, and she lay back on the sand willingly, reaching up to put her arms around him, her mouth opened softly in ecstasy. Slowly he unbuttoned the buttons of her blouse, then dropped gentle kisses down into the valley between her breasts.

She inhaled deeply, tightening her arms around him, feeling a rising tide of hunger sweeping through her. Some marvelously wild, sweet ache began deep inside, pulsing, insidious, impossible to control. He splayed his hand over her midriff and nuzzled his nose between her breasts, his breath warm and sweet against the lace of her bra.

"My God," he whispered. "You're so soft. You're like satin. Satin and silk."

She breathed in raggedly and opened her eyes. She felt drugged, almost sleepy, as if when he'd kissed her he'd placed her under a spell rather than brought her out of one. She reached up and ran her hand through his tousled hair. "Kiss me," she whispered.

His large body hovered over her, then he brought his head down, and her breath seemed to explode inside her. She tightened her arms around him, pulling him closer, feeling the intimacy of his weight on hers. He kissed her with delicious seduction, enticing and questioning. Softly he traced his tongue over her lips, and she moaned out loud.

"Let me put my tongue in your mouth," he whispered.

The spoken words seemed entirely too erotic. She moaned again and parted her lips, and he thrust his tongue deeply into her, sending spasms of desire oscillating through her body. Then he cupped her breast, and she felt the shock waves ripple through her body, felt heat explode in dizzying rivers as he brushed her hardened nipple with his thumb.

"Touch me," she whispered urgently. "Please, touch me."

He unclasped her bra and moved his hand underneath the thin lace, cupping her breast while his thumb moved in slow circles, sensitizing her so that she wanted to shout with ecstasy.

They lay like that, lost in rapture, the tide washing ever and ever closer until finally a great wave crashed ashore, washing over the sand castle and just touching her hair.

"The tide," she whispered raggedly.

"What about it?" he whispered back, his tongue moving in erotic circles around her swollen nipple.

"It's coming in," she said, hugging him tightly.

"Let it," he murmured, opening his mouth and sucking in her nipple, then swirling his tongue around it.

She gasped with pleasure, then gasped again when another wave sent water cascading under them, taking the very sand from beneath them and soaking them to the skin.

"Kyle," she said, laughing shakily, still sinking in pleasure, "the ocean..."

"Who cares about the tide?" he growled, throwing his leg over her and pressing himself intimately against her. He sat back and cupped her breasts in his palms, staring down into her eyes. "My God, you're beautiful."

She stared up at him, lost in wonder, while the sea inexorably moved closer and closer, enveloping them in briny lace. "We'll be drowned," she whispered.

"We're already drowning," he murmured.

She closed her eyes as he traced hot kisses down her neck, past the hollow of her throat, into the valley between her breasts, down and down, until he reached the waistband of her skirt. Slowly he gathered the material in his hands and pushed it up, then put his fingers in the waistband of her panties and tugged down.

At that moment a wave crashed over them, and they were covered. Spluttering and choking, they sat up and, as suddenly as it had begun, the mood evaporated. They sat, drenched to the skin, laughing and coughing.

"Are you all right?" Kyle asked, pounding her on the back.

She nodded, then laughed again. "I'm fine. You?"

"Perfect. I've never made love on the beach before." He grinned. "I want to do this with you every night."

She had to look away. Suddenly she was aware that she was half-naked. She clasped her bra and buttoned her blouse with shaking fingers. "I'm not sure that's a very good idea," she said in a low voice. "Don't they patrol these beaches at night?"

"I don't know. Do they?" Kyle stood up and tucked his shirt back into his trousers. "Who cares? Any policeman worth his salt would see we were enjoying ourselves and leave us in peace."

She stood up, grabbed the bottom of her blouse and wrung out the water, then shoved her hair back from her face. "More likely he would give us a ticket for indecent exposure."

"You have no sense of romance," Kyle teased softly, taking her into his arms and kissing the side of her neck. "No sense of daring or adventure."

"That's right," she said, primly pushing him away. "I'm a conventional girl with conventional tastes."

"You like it in bed, eh?" he asked, grinning. "That's okay by me. I'm willing to accommodate."

She glanced at him, then tossed her head. "Forget it, Frederick. Tonight was a momentary aberration. Blame it on the moon."

"The moon didn't have a damn thing to do with it and you know it," he said, his mouth still curved in a knowing smile. "Anyway, I just got a taste of what it could be like with you." He pulled her into his arms. "And now I want more. Lots more."

She stared up at him, not sure what to believe, then she pushed out of his arms. "I think we should go now," she said quietly.

He cocked his head and studied her intently. "Something's wrong."

She looked back at him. "It was nice, Kyle. You're a splendid lover, and frankly, it's been a very long time since I've...um...indulged, but that's it. No more. It's over."

"It's just begun. How can it be over?"

"It just is, that's all."

The corner of his mouth lifted wryly. "You really believe that, don't you?" he asked, shaking his head and beginning to chuckle. "What started tonight isn't over and it won't be for a long, long time. You and me, we're an item, Delta Daniels. It's only just begun."

Delta felt alarm tingle up and down her spine. She backed away from him, rubbing her arms. "No, Kyle," she said softly, pleading. "It can't happen again, ever." With that, she turned and raced toward the car, the wind whipping past her, taking hold of her hair and skirt, plastering her wet blouse against her suddenly shaking body.

Behind her, Kyle stood with his hands on his hips as he watched her run away.

Seven

Delta stood in front of the scale the next morning, feeling more apprehensive than she had in years. She forgot all about the lovemaking on the beach last night, forgot about her fears that Kyle was just romancing her to help her lose weight, and stared dry-mouthed at the scale.

She hated the damn thing. The scale had been her nemesis for years, prodding her when she needed to lose weight, taunting her when the weight wouldn't come off fast enough.

"Okay, Delta, the moment of truth," Kyle said, his clipboard in hand. He'd made up a weight chart for her and he stood ready to graph her exact weight in. It was Saturday, April 25. In less than two weeks, she'd appear on *Mornings with Morton*.

Delta glanced at Kyle apprehensively. "What if I haven't made my goal?"

He shrugged. "You'll just have to work harder this coming week."

"Work harder!" she wailed. "I'll die if I work much harder!"

"One of the nicest things about you, Delta," Kyle said, grinning, "is your tendency to underestimate calamities."

She glared at him, stepped onto the scale and prepared herself for the worst. Then she did a comic double take. "My glory," she said in awe, "does that say what I *think* it says?"

"One thirty-four," Kyle said proudly. "Bingo. You've gone under your goal by one pound."

"I lost six pounds," Delta said numbly, still staring at the needle, which sat squarely on 134. "I lost six *pounds*," she mumbled. She turned to Kyle and threw her arms around him. "Six pounds!" she shouted gleefully. "Oh, Kyle, I'm so happy!"

"Congratulation, Delta," he said, beaming at her. "I knew you could do it."

"But *I* didn't know it!" she said, eyes shining. "I've never taken off six pounds in a week before."

"You've never exercised this hard before, either. Exercise is the crucial difference, Delta—that and an almost fatless diet. Fat in the diet puts fat on the body. Leave out the fat, and you begin to lose weight fast. Add on exercise, and you lose it faster."

"Oh, stop being so logical and let me bask in my glory," she teased, still beaming.

"I'm proud of you, Delta," Kyle said, an admiring light in his eyes. "This week should prove even easier. You've got a good running start. Even if you only take off four pounds this week, you'll still be on target."

"But I want to lose five pounds!" she said. "Or six again. Let's see, that would put me at—" Her eyes grew enormous. "Oh, Kyle, that would put me at 128...."

"Shoot for five," he said practically. "Be grateful for four."

"Spoilsport!" she exclaimed, stepping off the scale. "I want to lose six, seven, eight pounds!"

"You will, but not in one week."

She shook her head at him. "You're raining on my parade, Kyle Frederick. You're the one who usually cheers me on."

"It's because I don't want you to get too discouraged if the weight doesn't come off as easily this next week. It's like that you know—it gets ornery."

"Yeah," she said, grinning. "Like certain men I know."

"I was thinking more along the lines of certain women I know," he said, chuckling.

"Call me ornery, I don't care," she said, throwing her arms out wide and bursting into song. "I'm in love," she warbled in an off-key soprano, "In love with the whole big wide world."

"Does that include me?" Kyle asked from just behind her.

She stopped singing. In her momentary joy she'd forgotten what had happened last night, forgotten that she'd responded to Kyle's lovemaking in such a way that he would certainly want even more. She turned slowly and looked at him. "No," she said quietly. "It doesn't."

He put the clipboard down and leaned back against the wall. "Last night you were pretty responsive."

"Last night I got carried away by the moonlight," she said, shrugging. "I told you it was a momentary aberration."

"Do you mean to say if I kissed you right now, you wouldn't respond?"

She darted him a nervous look, then nodded gaily. "That's exactly what I mean." She'd played poker before, and knew she had a pretty convincing act. She began to stroll along the Nautilus equipment, touching it lightly, talking over her shoulder as easily as if she were chatting about the weather. "I mean, it was nice and all, but really, Kyle, don't get the wrong idea. I'm a woman with all my hormones intact, so naturally I got a little carried away. But I'm not interested in continuing where we left off." She grinned at him over her shoulder. "Anyway, if we *had* continued, we'd have gotten a little wet."

"I like it wet," he said quietly.

His words acted like kerosene on a fire. She immediately lost all her nerve. Only she couldn't let him see that. Nervously she began to chatter. "You see, you're not really the type of man I'm attracted to, Kyle. I like men who are more..." She trailed off, her brain working frantically. "Well, more intellectual. I mean, you're very physical, and that's not really *me*, you see. I'm much more cerebral, if you want to put it that way. I like a man in a nice three-piece suit with horn-rimmed glasses. The Wall Street banker type. You're just not my type. I'm sorry, but that's the way it is."

She turned to smile apologetically at Kyle, only to have her heart fly into her throat. He was stalking her, coming toward her with slow, confident strides, amusement flickering in his eyes, one corner of his sculpted mouth lifted in indulgent humor.

"So you're not attracted to me," he said, his voice too low, too husky, threaded with dark irony.

"Th-that's right," she said, backing away, her voice breaking, her palms suddenly sweating. "I'm not."

"You like intellectual men," Kyle said, still stalking, seemingly in no hurry to prove her wrong. "Men who wear horn-rimmed glasses and three-piece suits."

She nodded, then forced out the words: "Y-yes, I do."

"And last night was a temporary aberration brought on by too much moonlight."

She nodded dumbly. She couldn't get any words out now. He was too close, too large, too magnificently attractive.

He reached out and traced his forefinger down her cheek, over the firm line of her jaw, then down her neck and into the hollow of her throat. "When I kissed you here last night, your pulse didn't pound, is that right?"

She could only nod, her eyes wide, her pulse screaming at her from just beneath his fingertip.

"You didn't feel anything inside," he murmured, his hand drifting over her breasts to rest on her stomach, "when I touched your breasts, and kissed them."

She took a ragged breath and shook her head, but she felt as if she were underwater. Her movements were sluggish, lethargic, as if her limbs were filled with hot, honeyed syrup.

"And if I touched you now," he went on, his voice even lower, huskier, "you wouldn't feel anything. No heat, no desire for me, nothing."

She nodded mutely, her eyes pleading with him not to do what he seemed to be threatening.

He slid his hands up her rib cage and cupped her full breasts in his palms. "So right now, when I'm touching your breasts this way, you don't feel anything, right?"

She couldn't move, couldn't speak. Her breath came quickly, raggedly, and she felt a slow, sweet languor steal over her, felt her nipples rising hard and urgent beneath his questing thumbs. Desperately she shook her head.

"Then why are your nipples getting hard?" he breathed softly. "Hmm?" He moved his thumbs back and forth over them, brushing, teasing through the soft material of her leotard.

She took a shaky breath and tried to push away, but he pushed her back against the wall and lowered his lips to the creamy curve where her neck joined her shoulder. "There's no moonlight now, Delta," he breathed, moving his tongue along the fragile ridge of her collarbone, nipping the soft skin with his teeth. "And I'm not wearing horn-rimmed glasses, either."

She rested her head against the wall, and her eyelids came down, shutting out the sight of him. But she couldn't shut out his smell or his touch. He enveloped her with a heady masculine aroma, invaded her with his probing thumbs and inquisitive tongue. His large body pressed against hers, sending her thoughts swirling in crazed circles.

Slowly she brought her hands up, intending to push him away, but instead she found herself exploring the leanly sculpted wall of his chest, found herself running her palms over the swelling muscles, then around his rib cage and up his back. She didn't even know what she was doing when she pulled his singlet from the waistband of his jogging shorts and ran her hands beneath it, up and over the firm flesh of his back.

"That's right," he breathed against her lips. "Touch me. Touch me everywhere, Delta."

As if hypnotized, she let her hands travel around to his chest, glorying in the feel of the wiry hairs there.

"Everywhere, Delta, the way I want to touch you," he whispered hoarsely.

She began to quiver. Slowly his hands moved down from her breasts, traveling in erotic pathways down her rib cage, then settling intimately on her hips. He pulled her against him and his arousal was immediately evident. She shook her head back and forth against the wall, her eyes still closed.

"No," she whispered.

"Yes," he sighed against her lips.

He inched his fingers beneath the leg of her jogging shorts, found the elastic of her panties, and ran his hands underneath to cup her buttocks. "You drove me crazy the other night in those overalls," he growled against her neck. "There's a hole in the back and I could see your skin. All night I wanted to kiss that little spot. What would you do if I kissed it now, Delta? Would you push me away?"

She was shaking, too weak to protest, too filled with desire. He softly kneaded her buttocks while his thumbs teased her, stroking her near the juncture of her legs.

"Let me touch you, Delta," he breathed.

She groaned and shook her head, eyes pressed closed as if she were in pain.

"Why not?" he asked, his lips brushing back and forth against hers.

She was going to die from this terrible, urgent need. She was going to faint, or maybe her knees would just buckle and she would slide down the wall into a neat little puddle on the floor.

"Oh, I see," he said, removing his hands from beneath her shorts and stepping back. "It's because I'm not your type of man, isn't it?"

She kept her eyes closed, struggling to regain her balance, to control the fire that was raging within her. She was humiliated, yet she couldn't find any anger to lash back at him with. It was even more humiliating to know that she just wanted to reach out for him, to pull him back into her arms and beg him to touch her, where she was trembling with need.

Finally she opened her eyes. He was standing, watching her, his face unreadable. "Tell me you didn't like it," he taunted softly.

She couldn't. She wanted to say it, but she couldn't. She continued staring at him, her eyes enormous, her breasts rising and falling in agitation, her body on fire.

"You can't, can you?" he asked. When she didn't respond, he repeated the question more sharply.

She shook her head, mute.

He nodded, then stepped even farther back. "All right. Just as long as we understand each other. You're attracted to me. It wasn't the moonlight and it wasn't any temporary aberration." His voice changed radically, going from seductive tenderness to harsh commands in ten seconds. "Now hit the floor, Delta. This week you're up to fifty sit-ups."

She blinked and stared at him, watching in confusion as he turned away. It took her about a minute, but she finally realized he wasn't going to kiss her any more. He expected her to get down on the floor and do fifty sit-ups. Disbelievingly she stared at him, then groaned and let her head drop back against the wall.

She couldn't do it. She couldn't last another minute without a dozen cookies or a cake. Somehow, in some way, she was going to have to get something to eat or she would just drop right here.

Delta stood with her nose pressed against the window of the Tidy Kake Bakery in Hyannis. There were huge trays filled with doughnuts and croissants and éclairs in the window, along with pies and cakes and loaves of bread. Her mouth watered and her stomach rumbled, and she looked around apprehensively, as if she expected someone to be watching, ready to pounce on her.

The worst thing about being a binger was the guilt. You felt as if you led a double life. You went into a bakery and smiled merrily when you bought a dozen doughnuts, pretending you were bringing them home to a large and loving family, when all along you were bringing them home to you, just you. Right now, standing in front of the window, her mouth watering, Delta felt as if the whole world knew her secret—that she was contemplating breaking her diet.

Distraught, Delta turned and hurried away, her heels clicking on the pavement, her face filled with torment. She couldn't give in. She couldn't. If she did, she would never forgive herself. She had gone more than a week without sweets, she could continue for two more weeks.

Trying to distract herself, she looked into a store window and caught sight of the reflection of a slender, attractive woman with short dark hair. For a moment she wondered who was walking next to her, then she realized it was her own reflection she was staring at.

She came to a halt, dumbfounded. She was actually almost slender! She was attractive...almost. She was—she gulped—she was almost *thin.* She turned to face the window and slowly walked toward it, watching the way her own body seemed to be approaching itself. When she got to the window, she reached out tentatively and touched her hand.

All she could do was stare into her own eyes, troubled beyond belief. Why was it so frightening to find herself attractive? Why did she immediately feel anxiety flutter along her nerve endings? She leaned her forehead against the store window and closed her eyes, seeing for the first time what her therapist and Kyle had been trying to make her see—she didn't *want* to be attractive. Being attractive was terrifying. If you were attractive, men might be interested in you, and if men were interested, then maybe you would have to get involved in a relationship, and if you got involved, you could get hurt.

Groaning, Delta opened her eyes, lifted her head and stared at herself. "You fool," she said softly. "You—"

She stared, remembering the times she'd heard Sheila say those exact words—Sheila with the exquisite face and flawless figure, with the golden hair and shining blue eyes—Sheila, who always seemed to be laughing at her.

Oh, you're such a klutz, Delta, Sheila would always say. Or *Look at Delta! Isn't she funny-looking? What man would ever want her? You better lose some of that weight, Delta, or no one will want to marry you. Don't be such a fool, Delta. Did you actually believe Jack Peterson loved you?*

Feeling sick, Delta turned and raced toward the bakery. She had to stop the memories, had to have the one comfort that God had given her. In her entire life there had been all kinds of negative voices, all kinds of criticism, but there had only been one source of comfort—food. It cuddled and cosseted her. It filled the hollow space inside her, the space that ached for love but got only sneering laughter.

She pulled open the door and stood at the counter, her heart pounding, her mouth dry.

"Afternoon," the woman behind the counter said, scratching her head with a pencil. "What'll you have?"

"Doughnuts," Delta said, hoping her voice didn't shake too much. "A dozen doughnuts." Now that she'd done it, she felt calmer. "A dozen chocolate-frosted doughnuts," she amended. "And a dozen sugar-frosted, and a dozen assorted."

"Gonna have a party?" the woman asked, grinning.

Delta raised calm eyes and smiled. "Yes," she said clearly. "I am."

Kyle sat in his pickup, staring at the door to the Tidy Kake Bakery, feeling sick inside. She'd been distraught, and something had told him to follow Delta when she left the house that afternoon. He shouldn't have done what he'd done, but a man could only take so much rejection. He'd only meant to prove to her that she cared about him, that she was attracted to him, but somehow he'd pushed her too far.

He knew there was something bothering Delta, something in her life that made her want to eat, but so far he hadn't been able to get close enough to find out what it was. He groaned to himself, cursing his stupidity. Every time he got close to Delta, his attraction to her surfaced and he found himself making a pass at her, which was obviously the worst thing he could possibly do.

He sat up. Delta was leaving the shop, her arms filled with boxes. He felt his spirits dip, felt all his belief in Delta begin to drain away in disappointment.

"Dammit, Delta," he said aloud, "couldn't you *talk* with me?"

He cursed himself and what he'd done both last night and today. No, of course she couldn't. She thought he was pretending to be attracted to her to help her lose weight. The problem was, he realized now, that a man's attraction was the very thing that would make her start eating again. If he wanted to help her, he would have to steer clear of the physical and focus on her as a person.

He groaned again, then slowly let out the clutch. He would follow her home and somehow convince her to throw out those pastries. In a single eating binge she could undo almost everything they had both worked so hard for all week. Then he saw her furtively sneak a look in the rear-view mirror, and he realized she wasn't even going to wait until she got home to start eating.

Delta's fingers shook as she opened the box of chocolate-frosted doughnuts. She stared at the doughnuts, her mouth watering, and chose the first in the row on the right. It was the biggest, with the most frosting. She looked in the rearview mirror and darted a glance outside, but no one seemed to be watching her. It wouldn't hurt to have a doughnut now before she drove home.

She took a huge bite of the doughnut and felt an immediate surge of gratification flow through her. Chocolate!

Lord, how she loved the stuff! She closed her eyes in ecstasy and chewed frantically, stuffing the doughnut into her mouth and reaching for another. Oh, God, it tasted so good. For a week she'd starved on celery sticks and lettuce, and now she was going to enjoy herself. She took another huge bite of the second doughnut and was reaching for a third when suddenly the door to her car was pulled open and she turned to find Kyle glaring at her.

At first she thought she was hallucinating—it was just her guilt complex overreacting—but then she realized it was really Kyle. She held the doughnut halfway to her opened mouth, staring into his eyes. They were a beautiful clear blue, and they were filled with disappointment. Slowly she lowered the doughnut and rested her head back against the car seat.

"You caught me," she said dully.

Kyle reached over her and picked up the box. "How many have you eaten?" He counted the two blank spaces and gently took the third doughnut from her hand. "I'll take that," he said. "No sense in going over your calorie limit."

Delta closed her eyes and turned her head away so that she wouldn't have to look at him, wouldn't have to see the disillusionment and disappointment in his face. She was always letting people down. She had let her mother down, and her sister. Her own father had died before she was born, but somehow she had even managed to feel responsible for that, too. And now she had let Kyle down. She heaved a tired breath and wished she could just disappear. Then her sense of humor surfaced and she began to chuckle.

"I was just wishing I could disappear off the face of the earth," she said, "but there's probably too much of me to disappear entirely."

"I'll take the doughnuts with me, Delta," Kyle said gently, ignoring her attempt at humor. "I'll meet you back at the house."

She sighed again and started the car. "I'm sorry, Kyle," she said, staring straight ahead, unable to meet his eyes. "I've let you down."

"No, you haven't," he said softly. "We'll talk when we get back home, okay?"

She lifted confused eyes. "Of course I let you down," she insisted. "I bought three dozen damn doughnuts! I let you down!"

He smiled, reached out a gentle finger and touched her upturned nose. "No, you didn't. Believe me, you didn't. Just drive home, honey, and we'll talk."

She sat in her car, staring unseeingly out the window, filled with something that felt strangely like heat but which was more comforting, more filling than any three dozen doughnuts could ever be. Turning her head, she watched Kyle walk toward his pickup, carrying the three boxes of doughnuts. She frowned as she watched him. His voice had been so gentle, so filled with kindness. Never in her life had she disappointed someone so badly and had them behave as Kyle just had. She couldn't understand it, couldn't fathom why she felt so... so *warm*.

She started the car and drove home, feeling a strange sense of calm. It must be the doughnuts, she told herself. It had to be the two doughnuts she'd gulped down before Kyle had found her.

Later, in her kitchen, she couldn't meet his eyes. Not that they were accusing. They weren't at all. In fact, it amazed her how kind they were, how filled with... what? Actually, now that she thought of it, his eyes seemed to be filled with something like forgiveness.

"I don't know why I did it," she said softly, still unable to look up at him. "I couldn't help myself, Kyle. It just built up inside like steam in a boiler and suddenly I just *raced* to get to the bakery and buy those doughnuts."

When he didn't say anything, she chanced a look at him and saw that he was frowning thoughtfully, studying the toes of his jogging shoes as he sat with his long legs stretched out in front of him. "What did you do with them?" she asked hesitantly.

He looked up at her then. "With what?"

"The doughnuts."

He smiled at her. "I threw them away."

She felt her heart dip. "You didn't."

"Sure did."

She groaned out loud. "Three dozen doughnuts," she said dully. "Gone."

"Two dozen and ten," he amended. "I imagine the sea gulls are having a ball. Put it down as a charitable expense, Delta. A wildlife contribution."

She sighed wistfully and rested her chin in her hand. "At least I got to eat two."

Kyle shoved her calorie counter sheet across the kitchen table. "Here, before we forget, better record the calories. I imagine that'll just about fill your chart for the day. You'll have to get by on water for the rest of the day."

She glared at him. Where was all that loving kindness he had displayed earlier? Suddenly he was the slave driver again, and she didn't like it. "Oh, come on, Kyle, let's just forget it, okay? I slipped, all right? I'm like an alcoholic—I fell off the wagon. Two lousy doughnuts won't hurt me."

"No, but three dozen might have," Kyle said quietly.

She had to look away from those blue eyes. Not that they were accusing. They were just direct. She sighed tiredly and pulled the calorie chart toward her. "Okay," she said irritably, "I'll record the damn calories."

"Good girl."

"Oh, stop good-girling me," she snapped, pushing the chart away. "Dammit, if you hadn't come along, I'd have been scarfing down a dozen chocolate-covered doughnuts right now."

"That's what's worrying me, Delta," Kyle said.

She glanced at him. "Yeah? Well, you don't have to worry anymore. I'm cured. I won't risk undoing all the good I've done again."

"I'm afraid I can't believe you."

She tilted her head, a disbelieving look on her face. "You what?"

"I said I can't believe you, Delta. I can't trust you. I'm going to have to do something drastic."

She stared at him, feeling worried for the first time. "What do you mean?"

"When you first hired me, Delta, I said I wanted complete control over your life. I also said that if you cheated on your diet, I'd quit."

She stared at him in horror. Oh, no, he couldn't *leave* her! Without him, she would go back to flab and fat in a matter of days. "But you said you wouldn't quit on me," she wailed softly. "You said—"

"I know what I said, and I meant it, but there's another way."

"Another way?" She frowned at him. What the heck was he talking about?

"There's only one way I can keep an eye on you to make sure you don't cheat again, Delta..."

She listened, but she didn't know what to expect. He was such a *strange* man sometimes. "Oh, yeah?" she asked. "What's that?"

"I'm moving in. From now on I'm here with you day and night, twenty-four hours around the clock. Is that clear, Delta? For the next two weeks, I'm your shadow."

Eight

She stared at him, bemused. For a minute there she'd almost thought he'd said he was going to move in with her. She sat back and laughed softly at herself, then stopped laughing when she saw the look on his face.

"You can't be serious," she said.

"I'm dead serious," he responded.

She stared some more, then shoved her chair back and catapulted from it. "Like hell you're staying with me," she snarled. "I won't have you invading my home, playing watchdog. Super Sleuth, the Fat Detector." She shook her head vehemently. "No. Is that clear? *No way.*"

"Then I go."

She put her hands on her hips. "You'd break your word?"

"Why not? You've already broken yours."

That stopped her. She heaved a frustrated sigh and scraped her hand back through her mop of curls. "But you can't just move in here," she said, pacing distractedly. "I mean, you just can't—" she made vague circles in the air "—can't . . . move *in*."

"Why can't I?"

"Well . . ." She laughed nervously. "Well, for one thing, it wouldn't look right."

"To whom? You don't have any near neighbors. I don't have anyone to answer to. You don't have anyone to answer to. We're both adults, free and clear. Who's going to be watching what we do, and who'd care even if they did watch?"

His logical answers stymied her. She gnawed on a thumbnail and tried to resist the picture of three dozen doughnuts sailing out of a pickup truck onto a deserted beach. Right now, she *needed* those doughnuts. "No," she said, shaking her head decisively. "It can't be done."

"It can be done."

"No, it can't," she insisted.

"Not only can it," he said, rising from his chair. "But it will be. Now, today, before another hour passes and you drive into town and buy out the local bakery."

"Look, today was a fluke, okay? I promise I won't do it again. Cross my heart and hope to die." She crossed her breasts, then held up her hand in the Girl Scout salute. "Scout's honor."

"No dice, Delta. The harm's done. You fell off the wagon and I'm going to make damn sure you don't do it again. I'll be back in an hour. If you so much as look at a picture of food, I'll break your lovely little neck." He smiled charmingly. "Is that clear?"

She straightened, meeting him eye to eye. "Perfectly."

"Good. Now hit the road for a five-mile jog. You need to work off those calories you just gobbled up."

"You *are* a slave driver," she cried, so frustrated she could spit.

He just grinned at her. "And aren't you lucky? Think *Mornings with Morton*, Delta," he said, walking toward the back door. "Think Marcia Howard and a big old needle, sewing your mouth shut. Think poverty. Think anything you want. Just don't eat anything.''

"Spoilsport," she yelled, but he'd already slammed the door and was gone.

It was unnerving, watching Kyle unload two suitcases from his pickup and carry them to the guest room just across the hall from her room. She stood warily in the hall and watched him unpack. It took him all of five minutes. He transferred neatly stacked gym shorts and underwear and other essentials into the dresser, zipped his suitcases shut, stored them in the closet, then turned to her.

"All settled. Did you jog?"

She gestured to her sweaty attire. "Can't you tell?"

"Five miles?"

She nodded wearily. "Yes, Kyle, five whole miles. I counted each step."

"Good." He rubbed his hands together energetically, then looked at his watch. "Well, what'll we do tonight?"

She fixed him with wry eyes. "*I'm* settling in a hot tub and soaking. I don't care what *you* do." With that, she turned on her heel, stalked across the hall and slammed her bedroom door. As the echo reverberated in the house, Delta swore under her breath and dreamed of chocolate éclairs and cream puffs, of a five-pound box of Carnaby Chocolate Creams, of hot fudge sundaes and banana splits....

"Delta?" A fist pounded on the door.

She glared at the door, determined not to respond. Dammit, this was *her* house, and she wasn't going to be bothered by an unwelcome houseguest.

"Delta?" The pounding came again, louder this time. "Dammit, if you don't open up, Delta, I'm coming in after you."

She debated what to do, then opened the door. "What?" she asked belligerently, her eyes glittering with anger. "Can't you leave me in peace for even five minutes? Do you always have to be bothering me?"

"We need to talk."

She folded her arms. "All right. Talk."

"Not like this." He looked around her room, then back at her. "I mean a real talk."

"Go ahead," she said shortly. "Really talk."

He muttered a low oath, then grabbed her hand and pulled her along behind him down the long hall to the stairs. They clattered down the stairs, Delta an unwilling participant in the journey as Kyle led her to her study.

"Sit down," he said shortly after slamming the door and herding her toward the couch. "We've got to get a few things straight between us."

She refused to sit. "I'll bet! That's an old line, Kyle. Did you think I'd invite you to stay in my room the next two weeks? Huh, Kyle? Is that why you're so angry? Because I didn't swoon all over you and ask you to sleep with me?"

"You are the most *irritating* woman," he said from between his teeth. "You—"

"I what, Kyle?" she jeered. "Don't I give your masculine ego enough strokes? Don't I simper enough, and bat my eyelashes at you enough?" She reached out and stroked his arm. "Don't I ooh and ahh over your muscles enough? Hmm, Kyle?"

"Don't push me, Delta," he warned.

"Push *you*, Kyle?" she asked widening her eyes in pretended innocence. She batted her lashes furiously. "But how could little ol' *me* push big ol' *you*?"

He bit off an oath and turned on his heel, putting the width of the room between them. He leaned against the wall near the fireplace, his arms folded. "Sit down, Delta," he said finally. "We have a lot to talk about."

She considered disobeying, but finally acquiesced. "All right," she said shortly. "I'm sitting. Talk if you have to, but make it snappy."

He sighed wearily and rested his head back against the wall, looking up at the ceiling as if praying for patience. Sighing again, he looked at her. "Delta, I care about you. I want to help you lose weight, that's why I'm here. But I think you need a lot more than exercises and a diet. I think you also need to talk.''

Dumbfounded, she simply stared at him. "Talk?" she said after finding her voice. "Talk about what? The weather? Sports? Nuclear disarmament?"

"About you," he said, his voice suddenly more gentle.

She tossed her head and began plumping up the pillows on the couch. "You're crazy. What the heck do we need to talk about me for?"

"To help you come to terms with your need to eat."

She snorted derisively. "You know why I eat, Kyle? To live. Simple as that. It's a matter of survival, pure and simple. Don't put any big psychological meanings to it, buster. It's biological, nothing more."

"I think you're right, partially. I think you do eat to live, but it's a psychological need you're feeding, not a purely biological one."

"Oh, fiddlesticks."

"What triggered your going into the bakery this morning, Delta?" he asked. "What were the thoughts you had that sent you running there?"

She heaved a tired sigh. "Oh, Kyle, come on, will you? I was *hungry*, dammit! I'd just spent an entire week subsisting on lettuce and celery. My body rebelled. It said feed me, so I did. Or at least I would have if you hadn't happened along."

"All right, let's examine that. If indeed your body was saying feed me, why did it ask for precisely that kind of food? Why didn't it ask for something more nutritious? It wouldn't have been so bad if you'd ordered some fresh sole and broccoli and pigged out on that."

"Pig out on broccoli?" she asked unbelievingly. "Come on, Kyle. One does *not* pig out on vegetables and fish. One pigs out, my dear, on junk food. Period."

"And why is that? Why do you need something that's not good for you?"

"Honey," she said wearily, "my body doesn't know what's good or not good for it, it only knows what *tastes* good. Doughnuts make the grade. Vegetables don't. Sorry, but that's the way it is in Fatso Land."

"You'd just weighed in and found out you'd lost six pounds. As I remember it, you were proud of yourself. Would that be likely to send you scurrying to a bakery on a binge?"

"Of course not!" she said heatedly. "I *was* proud of myself."

"Then what happened?" he asked softly.

She swallowed uneasily, unable to meet his eyes. "Nothing happened," she said finally.

"But something *did* happen, Delta. I kissed you, remember? I got you to admit you're attracted to me. I admit that I took advantage of your vulnerabilities to do that, but I couldn't help myself. Isn't that what did it, Delta? Isn't that what scared you so badly that you had to run to a bakery for comfort?"

She stared at the needlepoint pillow she held in her lap, then slowly let out a long sigh. "That's not it entirely," she said finally. "I was remembering some things, and I saw my reflection in a shop window, and—" She shook her head, confused by the jumble of thoughts in her mind. "Oh, Kyle, I don't know what it was. Maybe it wasn't just one thing, maybe it was twenty. All I know is, I did it and I'm sorry. I won't do it again."

"What things did you remember?" he asked.

She sighed tiredly. "I don't remember."

"Don't lie to me, Delta. How can we have a relationship based on trust if you lie to me?"

She gnawed on her lower lip, then threw the needlepoint pillow at a chair. "Oh, hell," she groaned. "I saw myself in a shop window and didn't recognize myself, then I kept hearing my sister, Sheila, jeering at me, telling me no one would ever love me." She picked up another pillow and held it to her, closing her eyes and beginning to sway back and forth, as if she were rocking a baby. "It's stupid, I know, but all my life Sheila's been the beautiful one, the one everyone admired. I was the clown, the one everyone laughed at."

"How do you feel about that?" Kyle asked gently.

She shrugged. "How am I supposed to feel?"

"I didn't ask how you're supposed to feel, I asked how you *do* feel. There's a difference."

She tossed the pillow away and stood up, beginning to pace the room agitatedly. She needed something to eat, something to chew on to calm her down. She pulled open her desk drawer where she usually kept a big box of Carnaby Chocolate Creams, but the spot was empty. Disconsolately she slammed the door shut and began pacing again, gnawing on her thumbnail.

"I'll tell you how I feel," she said, her voice shaking with emotion. "I feel rotten. All my life, I've been cute little Delta, the funny one. Then, when I brought Jack home—" She broke off suddenly, realizing too late that she'd almost spilled the beans.

"Jack?" Kyle asked mildly. "Who's Jack?"

She cursed herself roundly. "No one."

"He had to be someone," Kyle said, irritatingly logical. "You brought him home, after all."

"Okay, okay," she said grumpily. "He was a guy I knew at college, that's all. No one special."

"I think you're shading the truth a little."

She rounded on him. "Oh, just say it directly, Kyle. You think I'm lying."

He shrugged. "Okay, I think you're lying. I think he was important to you. Wasn't he?"

She sighed, feeling a strange sense of freedom. "Yeah," she said softly. "He was."

"You brought Jack home and something happened."

She stood at the sliding glass doors that overlooked the bay. "I brought him home and he saw Sheila, and that's all it took—just one look—and I could kiss him goodbye. Sheila struck again."

"What'd you do?"

"I went on my first binge," Delta said, still staring out at the bay, feeling strangely calm. "I ate and ate and ate." She turned and looked directly at Kyle. "Satisfied now? Happy, Kyle?"

"I'm happy you trusted me enough to confide in me. I'm unhappy for you though, Delta, because I know you must have really been in pain."

"Hey, I lived through it. Sheila and Jack were an item for a few months, then she dropped him. By that time I'd gained thirty pounds and Jack wouldn't even look at me."

"Maybe he couldn't look at you," Kyle said quietly. "Maybe he felt too rotten about what he'd done to you. Maybe he realized you were the one who really cared about him, and yet he'd fallen for looks. Maybe he felt pretty shallow."

Delta frowned thoughtfully, then shook her head. "Interesting interpretation, but I don't think so. He just wasn't interested in me anymore. I was fat."

"So fat equals safety, is that right, Delta?"

"No!"

"Then what does it equal?"

"Happiness."

"Uh-uh," he said, shaking his head and pushing away from the wall to stroll toward her. "I can't buy that. You sound as if you were pretty unhappy about Jack."

She frowned, trying to sort through the conflicting emotions inside her. "Okay, you're right. Fat doesn't equal happiness. Food does."

"I'd say it was more like food *compensates*. It doesn't equal happiness. It makes up for not having something. What do you suppose that something is?"

She closed her eyes and rested her head against the sliding glass doors. "Love," she said tiredly. "What else? Isn't it love that makes the world go round?"

"So, you're saying, when Jack fell for Sheila you lost the guy you loved and you compensated for it by eating and gaining weight?"

She frowned again, intrigued by Kyle's questions despite herself. "No," she said slowly. "It was more like I was *angry*, you know? And I couldn't express it, so I just got all my anger out by eating." She clenched her fists and felt the anger rise inside her, hot and devouring like flames. "I mean, I was so angry at Sheila—"

"What about Jack? Were you angry at Jack?"

She frowned again, puzzled. Was she? She shook her head doubtfully. "No, it was Sheila. I felt sad about Jack, but furious at Sheila."

"Why did you feel sad about Jack? Why weren't you angry at him? He was the one who betrayed you, after all."

"No, he didn't," she said. "He didn't have any more control of the situation than I did. He simply saw Sheila and fell for her." She snapped her fingers. "Just like that. Jack was as much a victim as I was."

"Victim," Kyle said thoughtfully. "Now that's an interesting word. And one other word you used interests me— control. You said Jack didn't have any more control over the situation than you did. So you felt helpless, is that it?"

She turned and stared at him. "What's all this about? Are you a shrink in gym teacher's clothing?"

"I'm your friend, Delta."

She stared into his eyes and saw the same warm kindness she'd seen in his eyes outside the bakery earlier today. Troubled, she rubbed her arms as if she were cold and walked away from the door. She began to wander the room, idly picking up a book here, then laying it down to pick up a trinket of some sort, only to put that down to pick up something else.

"You're restless," Kyle observed.

She shrugged and sighed. "Yes, I guess so."

"What are you thinking about?"

She paused, frowning, trying to get her thoughts in order. "What you just said about my not being in control of the situation."

"But you *are* in control when you eat, aren't you? I mean, you can make yourself gain weight, can't you? No one else can do that to you, can they?"

Puzzled, she turned and stared at him, her head cocked to the side thoughtfully. "That's interesting."

"Very. One of the most universal human needs is to be in control of our lives, not to be at the mercy of others. When you eat, you're in control, Delta. It's a magnificent defense mechanism. What you have to figure out is what you're defending yourself against."

She looked away from him. She already knew the answer to that, had discovered it today while staring at her reflection in the shop window. "I don't want to talk about this any more," she said.

"Okay."

She looked back at him suspiciously, but he seemed entirely happy to drop the subject.

"What *I* want to talk about is us, Delta," he said. "That's why I knocked on your door. I'm here for the next two weeks, and we have to figure out how we're going to coexist peacefully. I don't want the next two weeks to be nothing but shouting matches and power struggles."

She sighed and nodded. "Okay, how are we going to get along?"

"By being friends," he said. "I won't make any passes at you. I mean that, Delta. I'll treat you as a client and as a friend, nothing more."

For some reason what he had said was a horrible disappointment to her. She wanted him to make passes at her. She liked it when he kissed her, liked it that she felt attractive and desirable. Troubled, she worried her lip with her teeth. "All right," she said quietly. "I guess I can live with that."

Behind her, Kyle smiled to himself and folded his arms. It wouldn't be long, he thought, not long at all. She'd shown her disappointment at his words, though if she knew she'd shown it, she would be appalled—and angry. All he had to do was control himself around her for the next few days. He'd made important inroads, getting her to open up and

begin to talk at last about what troubled her. He would just
have to take it slowly, working with her every day, then
spending his free time with her. He still had to go to the gym
every day and take care of business there, but there would
be the nights....

He allowed himself the indulgence of a short fantasy—
himself and Delta, locked in loving embrace in her big bed,
then he shook himself. He couldn't allow that to happen,
not until she wanted it as much as he did. He sighed to himself and cursed his fate. Here he was with the one woman
he'd ever met that he wanted totally, and he was destined to
spend time with her as if she were merely a good buddy.

He watched her leave the room. Then he dropped tiredly
into a wing chair and just sat and stared thoughtfully out the
glass doors toward the bay. Her sister, Sheila, must be a real
beauty, and he didn't mean that literally. She sounded like
a self-centered egotist who didn't have the capacity to care
about others.

As difficult as it would be for Delta, he thought that confronting her sister would be the only thing that would help
her finally come to terms with her repressed anger and re-
sentment. Maybe then Delta would have a chance at happiness. But how could he convince Delta of that? From what
little she'd said, it sounded as if Delta would be perfectly
happy if she never saw Sheila again as long as she lived.

Frowning, he glanced around the room until his eyes came
to rest on an address book. Getting up, he flipped through
it until he found what he was looking for. Idly he tapped his
fingers on the desk surface, wondering just how he should
go about doing what he had in mind.

Nine

It felt strange having a man around the house. Delta had lived alone so long, she didn't know how to react to Kyle's presence. He sang in the shower—lustily. He whistled as he prepared her meals. He laughed uproariously at silly sitcoms on television. He was grumpy in the morning, for just a few minutes, then his naturally sunny disposition reasserted itself and he smiled cheerfully all day and into the night. The one thing he didn't do was make a pass at her.

Delta found this even more difficult to handle than his presence. She'd always known she was rebellious, but she hadn't expected to find herself rebelling at Kyle's friendly manner. For he was true to his word—he treated her as a friend and client, nothing more. As the days passed and he continued to maintain his cheerful amiability, Delta's mood plummeted from bad to worse. She who was usually cheerful and buoyant, who greeted every day with a fresh supply of jokes, began to be irritable. Kyle's constant cheer began to act on her the way acid acts on rust—it was wearing, to say the least.

But the most troubling problems were her inability to sleep at night and concentrate during the day. Images of Kyle invaded her dreams, keeping her awake into the small hours. During the day she found herself staring at him greedily, the way she once used to stare through candy shop windows.

She began to feel strange physical symptoms. At the sight of him she grew weak, then warm, then hot, as if her body were being invaded by a new and very potent strain of virus. Her body became ultrasensitive so that the pressure of her lace bra against her nipples drove her crazy. She would find herself lying in bed at night conjuring up the most exotic sexual fantasies involving Kyle, and while she was mortified by the fantasies, she had no desire to stop them. They left her feeling weak, hot and empty. Restlessly she would toss and turn and wonder what would happen if she got up and tiptoed across the hall.

The trouble was, she knew what would happen. Kyle would welcome her and all her fantasies would suddenly become real—but then life would get complicated. It always did when there was a man in the picture. She would want to eat like mad, and he would want her not to. They would be at each other's throats—not to mention the problems of appearing on *Mornings with Morton* looking like a stuffed sausage.

As a reward for having lost six pounds the first week, Kyle had upped her calories by two hundred, so she was able to add cereal with skim milk to her menu, doing away with the horrible concoction of hot water and lemon. On Friday morning Delta sighed over her bowl of cereal, wishing she was in the mood to enjoy it. Kyle glanced up at her from behind the morning paper.

"You feeling okay, Delta?" he asked.

She shrugged. "As good as a human skeleton can feel, I suppose."

"You're exaggerating again," he said, grinning.

She lifted irritated eyes and glared at him. "So? Exaggerating happens to be the one source of enjoyment left to me. I suppose you want to take that away, too."

"I wasn't aware I'd taken away all your sources of enjoyment," he said mildly, going back to perusing the paper.

Her mouth narrowed to a thin line and she considered throwing her bowl at him, then decided not to waste the last bit of milk from her cereal. Even if it was skim, it was better than hot water and lemon.

"What's left to enjoy?" she asked, taking up the subject where he'd left it. "You took away my food and you make me exercise. Now you want me to stop exaggerating." She shook her head dolefully. "Honest, Kyle, you're a royal pain."

"It's too bad those are your only enjoyments in life," Kyle said mildly, still looking at the paper. "Other women might find an opportunity for more...how shall I say it? For more *mature* pleasures."

Delta's spoon was halfway to her mouth, and it remained there, suspended in midair, as she stared at Kyle. Was he really getting at what she thought he was getting at?

"I beg your pardon?" she finally said after clearing her throat and assuming a carefully bored expression.

"I said other women, in the same situation as you, might find other enjoyable pursuits to occupy themselves with."

"Such as?"

He shrugged and folded the paper. "Learning a new sport, or taking long walks, or—" his blue eyes glanced off hers "—maybe something else physical."

"Such as?"

"Such as sex," he said.

"I *knew* you couldn't do it!" she crowed. "I knew you'd get around to propositioning me sooner or later. You must be the only jock in the country who scores in the bedroom more than he does on a ball field."

"I wasn't propositioning you, Delta. I was merely mentioning one other pleasurable pursuit that I haven't taken away from you."

"Oh, but you have!" she said, pouncing on his words. "You said you'd stay here but you wouldn't try anything."

"But that assumes you'd want sex with *me*, Delta," he said, raising his eyebrows to look a little surprised. "I was referring to other men. Surely you date."

"Not if I can help it," she said darkly. How was it that he could make her feel like a perfect jerk without so much as saying anything derogatory? It was as if he let her fashion her own noose from her own words, then hang herself. He was infuriating!

"Why not?" he asked. "What's wrong with an occasional date?"

"Because men...because I..." She sank into silence, then pushed back her chair. "Because I don't, that's all. Let's just drop the subject, okay?"

"Fine," he said, shrugging. "Whatever you say."

"My, aren't we amenable this morning," Delta said with false cheer. "Feeling frisky after our morning run, are we?"

"We sure are," he said with a grin.

She met his gaze directly, then looked away. Something hung in the air between them, and it wasn't anger. It was more like an electric charge, ready to explode. She turned her back and tossed her head, wishing she had a long ribbon of sleek black hair to toss over a sultry shoulder. Instead, she had to be content with a soft cap of quivering curls.

"You're supposed to say 'hrrumph,' Delta," Kyle said from just behind her.

She froze. He was too near, and she felt too vulnerable. Last night her fantasies had been particularly juicy, and she was close to the breaking point. "Why, whatever do you mean by that?" she asked innocently, then realized she sounded as false as a wooden nickle. He must be laughing at her behind her back. She decided it wouldn't hurt to look, so she turned around, then wished she hadn't.

He was closer than she'd thought. Much too close. She backed up as far as she could, which wasn't much, then stood staring up into his eyes. The problem was, they were beautiful eyes, mesmerizing in their intensity. And his mouth... Delta took a trembling breath and tried to tear her gaze off his mouth, but she couldn't. Unbidden, images of him kissing her entered her fertile imagination.

"Um..." She cleared her throat and inched along the counter, wondering how she could escape the magnetic field that seemed to envelop Kyle and snare her. "I..." Her voice broke, and she had to pause and clear her throat again. "Er..."

"Is something bothering you, Delta?" Kyle asked. His voice was full of solicitude, but his eyes were filled with amusement.

"No," she said, widening her eyes and shaking her head. "I was just thinking it's time for my Nautilus workout."

"That can wait," Kyle said softly. "Maybe you should try some other form of exercise."

"Other form?" she asked nervously, glancing behind him to try to ascertain how she might escape.

"Yes, you see, Delta, I've got a problem, a *big* problem."

Her eyes widened even more, but she didn't say anything. Was he hinting at what she *thought* he was hinting at? She shifted uneasily, uncomfortably aware that her nipples were erect beneath her soft T-shirt. "Well, just exactly how big is it?" she asked, then shook her head distractedly, her face beet-red. "I mean, just what kind of *problem* is it?"

He eased his left shoulder in pained circles, his right hand on it gently, and grimaced as if it hurt badly. "I think I wrenched my back last night down at the gym during my workout. I wondered if you could give me a massage."

Her mouth went dry. Oh, Lord, a massage. "Well," she said nervously. "I'm really not *trained*...I mean I don't know the proper techniques...I mean, I might hurt you even more." She stared into his eyes and said the next thing that popped into her head. "Sure, I'd be glad to."

Immediately after she'd said it, the color drained from her face, and she leaned weakly against the kitchen counter, wondering what demon had sprung into her brain at just that moment.

"Good," he said. "Tell you what, why don't you take a shower and I'll take a shower, then I'll meet you—" he looked around thoughtfully, then met her gaze "—in my room?"

She tried to think of a better place. She should suggest the study or the family room. Any place was better than his room. "Okay," she said, nodding cheerfully, then she wafted from the room, not sure she was sane, but damn sure she wasn't crazy.

Delta prepared herself as she would for her bridegroom. By the time she was finished her hair was gleaming, her skin was smoothed with lotion and her face glowed with a combination of excitement and subtle makeup. While perfuming the hollow of her throat, she remembered the way Kyle had kissed her there, and she felt nervous flutters attack her stomach.

Then she stood in front of her closet and debated what to wear. She decided on a pair of white shorts and a loose top with a low neckline that buttoned down the front. When she was dressed, she stared at herself in astonishment. Her clothes were actually big on her! She wadded up the extra material at her hips and held out the blouse, which suddenly looked like someone's hand-me-down maternity clothing.

"I don't believe it," she said out loud in awe, then darted for the back of her closet, where her "slim" clothes were stashed. She found what she was looking for way in the back. Reverently she took it off its hanger and held it up to herself. It was a floor-length hostess gown of turquoise silk, with a long zipper that ran down the front from neck to toes. She had outgrown it a couple of dozen times, but kept it because she felt so delicate and feminine in it. She knew she shouldn't wear it. It was a blatant invitation, but that little demon inside her insisted, and she couldn't refuse.

She put on her laciest bra and her laciest bikini panties and then pirouetted in front of her mirror, her mouth suddenly dry, her heart pumping wildly, her cheeks aflame with color. On a rare day Delta could admit she was attractive, and this was such a day. Her eyes seemed greener, her skin softer, her smile prettier. Even her hair looked good, shining and burnished with sun-ripened reddish highlights.

She took a tremulous breath and floated across the hall. She stood indecisively, then tapped on Kyle's door. "Kyle?"

She heard his bathroom door open, then he called out. "Come on in, Delta. I'll be right out."

She opened the door hesitantly and saw that his bathroom was filled with steam, but Kyle was nowhere in sight. His cheerful whistling came from behind the half-opened bathroom door, so she presumed he was dressing behind the door.

Relaxing slightly, she wandered toward a window and stood looking down at the sliver of Cape Cod Bay that was just visible beyond the salt marshes. In the past two weeks, the forsythia buds had begun to swell, and daffodils were still nodding lazily in the breeze. There was a hint of real spring in the air—the sky was brighter, the air warmer, the sun higher in the heavens. She took a deep, satisfied breath. At least there was one thing about her life she didn't regret—she loved living on Cape Cod. It was the most beautiful place on earth, especially now, before the tourists poured over the two silver bridges that linked it to the mainland of Massachusetts.

"It's a beautiful view, isn't it?" Kyle asked softly.

She turned in surprise, then went very still. He wore only a white towel wrapped securely around his middle. Other than that scrap of terry cloth, he was naked, and a more beautiful naked man she'd never seen. On his muscular chest there was a feathering of soft hair descending into a line that disappeared beneath the waistband of the towel. His body was like sculpted steel.

Delta took another tremulous breath and let it out on a drawn-out sigh. "Well!" she said, trying to sound bright and chipper and failing miserably. "Looks like you're all set."

His eyes swept down her, then up again. "You look beautiful, Delta," he said softly. "You should always wear that color."

She smiled, feeling suddenly radiant. It was a miracle what a few words spoken by a man could do for a woman's ego. "Two weeks ago," she said, swirling around, "it didn't fit. Now it does. I have you to thank for that."

He shook his head, smiling at her. "You've done it all, Delta. I've just stood by and been a general nuisance."

Her smile faltered, and suddenly she felt awkward. "Well," she said slowly, "I guess we should get started."

Kyle nodded. "There's some lotion in the medicine cabinet. I always find a back rub feels nicer with lotion."

She nodded abstractedly and watched as he lay on his belly across his big bed. She felt an immediate tidal wave in her stomach, so she dashed into the bathroom and slid open the medicine cabinet door. Then she stood hesitantly, staring from her reflection to the bottle she held in her hands.

"Did you find the stuff, Delta?" Kyle called out.

"Yes," she called back, but continued to stand and stare at herself.

A minute passed, then Kyle called out again. "Well? Are you coming in here, or do I have to come in and get you?"

"I'll be right out," she called, then took a trembling breath and told herself to stop being so frightened. All she was going to do was give the man a back rub. What could be more innocent than that? She suppressed a low groan in response to the silliest question she had ever asked herself, then forced herself to enter the bedroom.

He was lying on his stomach, his head cradled on his folded arms, his eyes closed. He'd loosened the towel so that it was draped across his rear end, but no longer fastened. At the sight of it Delta's heart went into palpitations. She approached the bed slowly, then sat on the edge and stared at his magnificent back. She felt an intense desire to touch him, and realized with relief that she could touch him all she wanted, legitimately—she was about to give him a back rub.

She poured a little lotion into her hands and rubbed it in circles to warm it up. "This might be a little cool," she said softly, then began applying the lotion in large circles onto his smooth back.

"Feels good," he murmured drowsily.

She felt her breath catch in her throat and nodded silently in agreement. It did feel good. His skin was as smooth as satin, and was warm as a sun-toasted beach. She rubbed the lotion in, feeling mesmerized by the motion of her hands, loving the feel of his smooth skin. Slowly she began to knead the muscles at the top of his shoulders and around his neck, then she ran her thumbs down his spine to his waist before sliding her palms up his back to begin the entire process all over again.

Little by little she felt the tension ease out of his muscles, sensed his complete relaxation. Strangely, as he relaxed, so did she, as if the act of massaging his aching muscles released her own tension. She found herself smiling dreamily, humming softly as she massaged and smoothed her hands over his back.

"This is nice," she said softly, still smiling dreamily.

"Yes, it is," he echoed, then rolled over.

She found herself staring down into the bluest eyes she'd ever seen. They seemed darker than the stormy waters off the Cape, bluer than the sky on a bright October day. Without thinking, she reached out and rubbed her palms over his chest.

"You have the nicest skin," she murmured.

He ran his hand up her arm under the the voluminous sleeve of her gown. "You do, too."

They continued staring into each other's eyes, then he tugged gently on her arm, coaxing her forward. "Come here," he whispered.

She hesitated and he tugged again. "Delta," he whispered, "kiss me."

She couldn't resist. She wasn't made that way, didn't have steel in her backbone or ice in her veins. She leaned forward and kissed him softly, hesitantly, then let her lips hover just above his.

"That was nice," he breathed. "Do it again."

She hesitated, so he raised himself and touched his lips to hers, softly, as gently as a raindrop kissing a rose petal, then he lay back down. "I love to kiss you," he murmured, his hand rubbing her arm beneath the sleeve of her gown. "You taste like peaches and cream."

Her breathing had quickened as her body began to respond to his. She stared into his eyes, feeling heat rise in her like steam from a sizzling sidewalk. "I like to kiss you, too," she whispered.

"Then do it again."

She almost didn't, and he must have sensed her reluctance, for he put his arms around her and dragged her down to his chest, running a hand through her hair and holding her head to his, then exploring her lips lazily, luxuriating in her, as if they had all the time in the world.

She melted against him, losing the last of her fear along with her inhibitions. He was too masculine, too vitally attractive to fight off any longer. She ran her hands over his chest and exhaled softly when at last their lips broke apart.

"Oh, Kyle," she breathed, her eyes closed in rapture. "Kyle..."

"I love the way you say my name," he whispered, lifting his head to drop kisses along her collarbone. Gently he tugged on the zipper, and her gown fell open. His lips followed, gliding sensually over the lace of her bra into the valley between her breasts, then over her midriff, sending delicate shivers of delight cascading over her sensitive skin. He stopped kissing her at the top of her panties, but he kept unzipping the gown until it was fully open and she lay exposed to his seeking eyes.

"You're so beautiful, Delta," he breathed.

She lay there, looking at him, feeling an incredible rush of desire flood through her, breaking over her like hungry waves on a storm-tossed coast. "Touch me," she whispered softly. "Kyle, please touch me."

He unclasped her bra and gently removed it, along with her gown. Then he began kissing her breasts, cupping their fullness in his palms, manipulating the rising tips of her nipples with his thumbs.

She swam in delicious waters, feeling desire ripple through her on ever-mounting waves. Heat coursed through her while ecstasy danced around her. She felt as if she'd been wandering in a desert for dozens of years, but now she'd happened upon an oasis. His touch and his kisses brought her to life as surely as water gave life in the desert.

She put her arms around him and simply held him. If she could hold him like this forever, she thought, she would never need to eat anything again as long as she lived—no food, no doughnuts, not even any silly Carnaby Chocolate Creams. Everything she needed was here with him. He completed her. She had been half-alive all these years, and now she was whole.

Only one frontier remained to be explored. She felt herself growing progressively more ready for lovemaking, yet he persistently refrained from touching her where she most needed his touch. Slowly she reached out and took his hand, guiding it to her.

"I want you to touch me," she whispered, her eyes enormous as they looked into his.

His breath exploded in a tortured sigh, and he buried his head in her breasts while cupping the soft mound of her womanhood. "It's what I've wanted for so long, Delta," he murmured. "I was afraid you'd never want me enough."

"I want you," she whispered.

He edged her panties gently from her hips, sliding them down the length of her legs and tossing them aside. Then he moved his hand between her legs and began a slow massage that made her senses scream out for relief. Her hips began a methodical back-and-forth movement, which increased as his fingers quickened. She felt flooded with beauty, drowning in sensation, filled with incredible heat that mounted to

a frenzied height, then stayed poised on the brink of release.

"Delta," Kyle crooned softly, "you are so beautiful, so
desirable."

His words startled her, bringing her abruptly back to
reality. Suddenly the release that had seemed so imminent
was denied her. Instead of mounting desire, she felt fear rise
inside her like a great black cloud blotting the sunshine from
her sky. She wasn't beautiful and she wasn't desirable. He
was just saying that, using all the techniques he could mus-
ter to achieve his aim—to help her lose weight.

Her initial joy at his touch drained away completely, and
she pushed his hand away and turned on her side, putting
her back to him.

"Delta," he asked, his voice filled with concern.

She didn't speak; she couldn't. Fear held her in its grasp,
destroying all hope.

"Delta," he said said softly, putting his arms around her
and pulling her back against his chest. "What is it, honey?"

She closed her eyes against the tears that threatened to
overflow, then got up hurriedly and put on her gown. Her
fingers shook as she zipped it up. Then she snatched her
underwear from the floor where Kyle had tossed it and
started to hurry from the room.

Kyle caught her at the door. "Don't go, Delta," he said
softly. "Stay here and talk to me."

She refused to look at him, couldn't trust that what had
happened between them had been real. "There's nothing to
talk about," she said. "I have to do my Nautilus routine
now or my fitness trainer will be angry," she continued in a
poor attempt at humor.

"The hell with your fitness trainer," Kyle said almost
roughly. "What about *me*?"

She looked at him then, so surprised at the hurt in his
voice that she had to. What she saw astonished her: he *was*
hurt. He perceived her leaving as some sort of rejection of
him.

Suddenly she wondered if she really knew anything at all about anything. Maybe Kyle really did care for her. Maybe his attention wasn't a ruse to get her to lose weight, to keep her from overeating. Troubled, she stared into his face and automatically reached out to him, caring more for him now than for herself.

"I'm sorry," she said softly. "I'm just frightened, Kyle."

"Oh, honey," he breathed. "Don't be afraid. Don't ever be afraid with me. I won't hurt you, Delta."

The tone of his voice reached her. She felt something inside relax, some fear that had held her back all these years, haunting her with its intensity.

"I'll try, Kyle," she said softly. "I promise. From now on I'll try."

He gathered her gently in his embrace, holding her as if she were treasure. "That's all I ask, honey," he murmured to her. "Just leave the rest to me."

She closed her eyes and relaxed against him, feeling she had arrived in a safe harbor for the first time in her life.

Ten

___

The next day Delta weighed in again and found to her delight that she had lost another five pounds. She had broken through 130 pounds and rested comfortably at 129.

"That's eleven pounds in just two weeks," she said, beaming at Kyle. "I can't believe it! That means I only have to lose four more to make my goal by next Friday!" She looked at him anxiously. "Do you think I can do it?"

"Of course you can do it," Kyle said. "I have absolute faith in you."

She sighed uneasily. "Well, I'm glad someone does, because I sure don't."

"Hey, where's that happy face I saw just a few minutes ago? Already you're predicting gloom and doom. Relax, Delta, you're on your way. Next Friday you'll be on *Mornings with Morton* looking smashing, and your book will be even more successful than it is now."

She smiled at him gratefully. "You really are a good fitness trainer," she said softly. "You make me feel as if I *can* do it."

"But you can, Delta. You always could. It's keeping the weight off that's been your downfall, but I think we'll whip that, too. I don't think you're ever going to have to be on a diet again."

"Oh, Kyle," she said, nervous at the mere prospect of no more seesawing on the scale. "Don't get your hopes up. I'll probably fall off the wagon the moment I leave the television studio next Friday."

"Another thing we have to tackle with you, Delta, is your negative thinking. Come on now, think positively. Of *course* I'm going to get my hopes up. Hope is all we have in life, Delta. It's what keeps us going."

She felt herself begin to smile. Listening to Kyle was always a revelation to her. Invariably, whenever he talked with her, he left her feeling better about herself. She realized in a sudden flash of insight what a tremendous gift it was to make a person feel better about themselves, rather than worse.

Suddenly she remembered Sheila and how her sister had the knack of constantly downgrading her, of criticizing and carping and destroying her innate optimism. Delta frowned thoughtfully, wondering for the first time if some kind of unhappiness in Sheila's life had made her act that way. Maybe Sheila had attacked Delta not out of spite, but out of her own unhappiness.

"You're looking mighty thoughtful," Kyle said.

"I was thinking about Sheila," Delta said. "You know, it suddenly hit me that she might not be very happy."

"Oh? What made you think that?"

"I'm not sure. I think I just got a glimpse of something. I think when people constantly criticize and complain, maybe they're really just very unhappy themselves." Delta's frown grew. "But that doesn't make any sense," she said slowly. "I mean, Sheila's absolutely beautiful!"

"And you think beauty is a guarantee of instant happiness?" Kyle asked.

Delta glanced at him thoughtfully. "I always have."

He smiled ruefully. "Once, a long time ago, I thought that fame would guarantee me happiness. It didn't, and money didn't."

"What did?"

He sighed restively and scraped a hand back through his hair. "I guess I finally just realized that happiness isn't something you pursue. It finds you when you're ready for it."

"Then I guess there are an awful lot of people who aren't ready for it," Delta said sadly.

Kyle nodded. "Yes, I'm afraid so. But I firmly believe happiness is something that each and every one of us can find. We just need to face whatever holds us back. For some of us it's our fears about the way we look, or about how we failed once, or about how we're not loved. Once we face ourselves squarely and stop running from the truth about ourselves, I think that's the beginning of finding happiness, Delta."

"It's all just peace of mind, then?"

"Yeah, I guess that's what I mean. Happiness is being able to accept yourself for what you are. The minute you do, you find what you'd been searching for outside yourself for so long."

Delta stared at Kyle, then smiled slowly. "You're a nice man, Kyle," she said softly. "Did you know that?"

"Well, it's always nice to be told," he said gently, smiling at her.

She felt warmed down to her toes. Impulsively she put her arms around him and hugged him tightly. He responded by laughing easily and hugging her back. Suddenly she felt safe and warm and protected, as if she'd stumbled into heaven while looking for something else entirely.

"I think you deserve a reward for making your goal," Kyle said softly.

"A reward?" she asked, brightening. "What kind of re-ward."

"Well, certainly not Carnaby Chocolate Creams," Kyle said dryly. "I was thinking along the lines of a night on the town with me."

She felt as if she were glowing. "I think that would be a wonderful reward," she said softly.

"Then put your prettiest dress on," he said, grinning, "because tonight we're going to paint the town red."

"And how do you plan to do that?" she asked, laughing.

"We'll start by going out to eat," he said. "It's time you began a more realistic diet. I've had you on strict rations up until now, but it's risky losing weight this fast. We have to start you on a healthy diet, one that allows you to enjoy food but not gain weight." He smiled, and a devilish gleam entered his eyes. "Then we'll see what else the evening brings. Maybe we'll go dancing again, or build sand castles on the beach, or..." he trailed off, his eyes growing dusky with heat. "Or maybe we'll just come home and spend a little time together."

For a moment Delta was worried. Kyle seemed to be hinting that perhaps they would end up making love, and she wasn't sure she was ready for that. Then she told herself to stop worrying and begin trusting Kyle a little. So far, he'd never done anything to make her *not* trust him.

"Okay," she said softly. "That sounds fine."

"Good." Then he was all business. "Now how about a hundred sit-ups? We want that stomach of yours as flat and hard as an ironing board."

"You would," she groaned. "Just when I was beginning to think there was more to life than jogging and working out."

"There is," he said, eyes gleaming. "But not until you reach your goal next Friday."

Somehow that relieved her. It sounded as if Kyle wouldn't try to pursue anything further until after she'd appeared on *Mornings with Morton*. A tiny suspicion flitted in and out of her mind that maybe he would disappear completely after she'd reached her goal and appeared on the television show, but she squelched the doubt. What had Kyle just said about negative thinking? She would have to begin trying to practice what he preached, and it wouldn't hurt to start by assuming that he really *was* interested in her for herself.

Her eyes grew wide and her mouth watered at the sight of the menu that night at dinner. "I'll have one of each entrée," she said, laughing with Kyle. "And three desserts."

"I recommend fish, broiled without butter but with a little lemon," Kyle said. "And fresh vegetables, no rolls or butter, perhaps a light salad with low-cal dressing, and a glass of wine."

Sighing, Delta felt as if she were in heaven. Even that lean fare was more than she had had the past two weeks. She felt pampered and spoiled, as if she were indulging in epicurean feasts that would have shamed the Roman emperors.

She looked around approvingly. Kyle had chosen one of the nicest restaurants on the south side of the Cape. Overlooking a harbor, it sported pink linen tablecloths, white bone china, orchids in crystal vases and candles at each table. A string quartet played quietly in the background, adding to the general ambience of restrained elegance. Outside the wall of windows, the Atlantic Ocean rolled onto the beach, scattering white lace bubbles over the slick expanse of wet sand, then dragging shells and tiny stones back into the water in its wake.

"You look lovely tonight, Delta," Kyle said, his eyes only on her.

She flushed and dragged her gaze away from the view. "I feel lovely," she confided, then laughed in embarrassment. "Well," she qualified, "I mean, I'm enjoying myself."

"I liked it better when you said you felt lovely," Kyle said, his tone serious, his eyes catching and holding hers. "But I like the idea that you enjoy being with me. I hope you've gotten over that ridiculous notion that I'm only going out with you to make you feel better about yourself and lose weight. There must have been other men in your life."

She nodded, sipping the wine Kyle had ordered for her. "There have been, but every time I start getting involved, I begin to gain weight." She looked up and met his gaze. "You're helping me see there's a connection."

"Which is?"

"That I'm afraid of getting involved."

He nodded, sitting back and toying with his glass of Scotch. "Why do you think that is? Does it have something to do with what happened with Jack Peterson?"

Startled, she stared at him. To the best of her knowledge she'd only mentioned Jack once. She shrugged carelessly. "Who cares? That's all in the past."

"That's right," Kyle said, "and we're in the present." He sat forward and began tracing his fingertips over the back of her hand. "How do you feel about getting involved with me?"

She stared down at his hand, then lifted wide eyes. "Scared to death," she said truthfully. "I'm afraid I'll start eating again."

"Go out of control, you mean," he said.

"Exactly."

"But I'll be with you all week. I won't let you begin eating."

"Yes, but what happens after that?" she asked, frowning. Then she shook her head. "I don't know, Kyle. Maybe I'm not meant to get involved with men. Maybe I should just resign myself to being slim and celibate or fat and..."

"And what?"

She began to grin. "Fat and happy," she said, resting her chin in her hand.

He grinned back, resting his own chin in his hand. "What if you could be slim and happy?"

She sighed wistfully. "That'd be heaven."

"So who says you can't have heaven on earth?"

"Experience," she said wryly. "I've tried a couple of times and it never worked."

"Maybe this time it will."

She sighed again, feeling slightly dreamy. "You're a very attractive man, Kyle Frederick," she said, smiling slowly. "You make a very good case for getting involved with you."

"After dinner I intend to make an even better one."

She felt her stomach turn upside down, then right itself. "Careful," she cautioned softly, "you just might make me ravenous. I'm in a restaurant, remember. This is akin to letting a pyromaniac into a match factory."

"Being ravenous is okay with me," he drawled. "Just make sure your appetite's for me."

Her stomach flip-flopped again, and she had to take an unsteady breath to calm herself. "I don't think there's any problem there," she said, sounding breathless. "In fact, for the first time in my life that I can remember, I'm not even thinking about food in the presence of a man."

"What are you thinking about?"

"You," she answered after a short pause. "And that back rub I gave you yesterday."

His eyes seemed to grow darker, and suddenly he looked restless, as if this restaurant were the last place he wanted to be. "I didn't reciprocate, did I?" he asked at last. "Now that was downright inhospitable of me. If you'll forgive me, I'll make that up to you tonight and give you a back rub you'll never forget."

She felt deliciously dizzy, and couldn't seem to keep from drowning in his eyes. "That sounds nice."

"Yes," he said huskily, "it does. So nice that I don't think I want to eat this meal. I just want to take you home and carry you to bed."

Her sense of humor returned. "It's a good thing I lost some weight," she said wryly, "or you'd get a hernia trying."

One corner of his mouth lifted, and he shook his head, his eyes admiring. "I'd make it," he said. "You never weighed that much that I couldn't pick you up and carry you to the nearest bed."

"No," she said flippantly, "but you might not have wanted to if I hadn't lost that weight."

"Not true," he countered. "I wanted to that first day I set eyes on you. Your weight never entered into it. Some things, like mating, are instinctive. You find the right woman and nature takes over."

"And am I the right woman, Kyle?" she asked, suddenly serious again.

"You're as close as I've ever come," he said, just as seriously.

They sat and stared at each other, then she dropped her gaze from his, confused. Things were going too fast, and she didn't know what to believe. The only thing she knew was that she liked the way he made her feel. For a moment it startled her that love could be so simple. Wasn't it something you worked at, that took months to develop, that was tested over time? Wasn't instant physical attraction untrustworthy? Shouldn't she be running instead of sitting here getting deeper and deeper into something she wasn't even sure about?

The thing of it was, though she was unsure, she wasn't unsure. It didn't make sense and wasn't logical, but something deep inside felt *right* with Kyle. She had her share of doubts, and more than her share of fear, but that didn't seem to matter in the end. All that mattered was being with Kyle. In comparison, nothing else in her life seemed as important.

Then she remembered *Mornings with Morton* and Marcia Howard and she realized that at least one other thing was important—her career. And her career depended on her losing weight, which was where Kyle Frederick came in.

Or was it? Kyle may have entered her life for the express purpose of helping her lose weight, but she had a hunch he was in it for other, more important reasons now. She felt as if she were at a crossroads, that she had reached some important place in her life where she would have to make a decision. She could continue walking the same road she'd been on since that eventful weekend when she'd brought Jack Peterson home, or she could change her life completely.

Suddenly she was afraid, heart-stoppingly afraid. The old way might have been painful, but at least she was familiar with it. A new way of living would entail all sorts of changes, and maybe she couldn't make those changes. She was thirty-two, after all, not exactly young. She'd been in a rut for years. Who said she could break old patterns now?

The waitress came and set her plate in front of her. She lifted her gaze from it and looked at Kyle. She had a choice—food or Kyle. Suddenly she was ravenous, filled with hunger such as she'd never experienced in her life. She picked up her fork with shaking fingers, and plunged it into the succulent swordfish steak. The first taste was almost a shock. The lemon-basted fish wasn't what she needed. She needed something sweet—a boxful of Carnaby Chocolate Creams perhaps, or cookies or a half gallon of ice cream.

"You're looking nervous," Kyle said quietly. "Are you okay?"

She took a shaky breath and put down her fork. "Sure," she said cheerfully. "I just haven't had so much food in a couple of weeks. I'm kind of enjoying it, that's all."

"Are you sure?"

She lifted her gaze, suspecting that he somehow knew what she was going through. "Sure I'm sure," she said, smiling gaily. "What else could it be?"

"Fear," he said. "Maybe all this talk about going home and my giving you a massage has frightened you all of a sudden."

She shook her head and picked up her fork again. "Uh-uh," she said, spearing a baby carrot. "I'm fine."

"Don't lie to me, Delta," Kyle said softly. "I can deal with the truth, but I can't deal with deception."

She kept her gaze on her plate, seeing a towering chocolate cake in place of the fish and vegetables. She blinked, then slowly put her fork down. "All right," she said quietly. "I am a little frightened, I guess. I'm not seeing fish and vegetables right now," she admitted. "I'm seeing chocolate cake and ice cream and doughnuts." She lifted her gaze to Kyle, her eyes wide with fear. "Kyle, I'm afraid I can't do it. I'm afraid I can't stop the need to eat. It's inside me, Kyle, tearing at me. This fish..." She trailed off, feeling helpless, as if she were in the grip of some terrible addiction. Tears sprang into her eyes and she shook her head, feeling suddenly lost. "It's no use," she whispered. "I can't do it. I'm not strong enough. It takes willpower to diet, and I haven't got any."

Kyle reached across the table and took her hand in his. "It's okay to be frightened, honey. That's part of the process. But don't give up now, not when you're so close. That's the reason you feel this way, you know—because you're close. You're real close, Delta. You've almost made the decision to stop overeating and take control of your own life, and that scares you. Well, it's okay to be frightened, but you can't let that fear rule you, Delta. You've got to face it and put it behind you."

She stared at the tabletop, but his words slowly reached her. Finally she lifted hopeful eyes. "I don't know, Kyle. I'm just not sure."

He squeezed her hand. "Come on, let's get out of here," he said, signaling the waitress for the check. "I think I know a way to convince you."

She shook her head, again filled with incredible anxiety. "It's never worked in the past," she said. "Being with a man has always sent me flying back to food."

"Not this time," Kyle said confidently. "This time it's going to be different."

She shook her head, still not convinced. "Why?" she asked sadly. "What makes this time so different?"

He met her gaze squarely. "Because this time the guy's in love with you, Delta, and love makes all the difference in the world."

She sat and stared at him, feeling oddly bemused. Had he just said those words, or had she imagined them? People didn't just sit in a restaurant and say they loved someone they'd practically just met. They waited a few months at least and said it on a romantic moonlit night with red roses at hand and glasses of champagne.

"I don't believe you said that," she finally said.

"I know you don't," he answered, "so I'm going to prove it to you."

He pulled her chair out, and she supposed she rose from it, and somehow they left the restaurant—though it was all a fog to her—and she guessed they walked across the parking lot and got into the car. At least that was where she found herself. She was sitting in the car and Kyle was driving, and there was music playing on the radio, but really, it was all still a blur, or a fantasy. Maybe she would wake up in a minute and find out she was dreaming.

She turned her head and studied him, taking in his clean-cut profile, the strength of his hands on the steering wheel, the fitness of his body under his sport jacket and slacks. She felt as if she were seeing him for the first time. For some reason the words he'd said in the restaurant had changed everything. Suddenly her entire life seemed new, as if she were viewing everything from a slightly different angle. Odd, how a few words could alter irrevocably the perspective from which a person viewed life.

"You're being very quiet," Kyle said, looking at her.

She nodded thoughtfully. "I'm thinking."

"Anything you want to share with me?"

She thought about that, then shook her head. "No, not really. I . . . I'm not ready to yet."

"Okay," he said.

She turned to study him again. "I don't understand you, Kyle. How can you say something like that when you don't even know me?"

He shrugged. "I know what I feel. Love is really very simple if you don't complicate it with a lot of fear."

"Fear?" She stared at him. What did he mean by that?

"Someone told me once that fear is the opposite of love," he explained. "At first, I didn't quite understand. If you'd asked me what was the opposite of love, I'd have said hate, but then I slowly began to understand it. Love is a positive force that works good in our lives. Fear is a negative one. It holds us back. If we go with the positive, if we trust our feelings, then we almost never make mistakes. It's when we begin to doubt that we get into trouble. And doubt comes from fear.''

"Do you really think love is so simple?'' she asked softly. "To me, it's always been so complex, so—" she searched for the right word "—difficult.'' She frowned, trying to explain. "All you have to do is look around. You see marriages breaking up, lovers quarreling, families split in two by individual needs that rise up and swallow all the love that once held them together.''

"But the problems don't stem from love, Delta," Kyle said softly. "They come from people not acting lovingly, from needs and wishes and our own human failings, but not from love.''

"You're an incurable romantic," she accused.

"That's right," he agreed happily. "I am." He took her hand and brought it to his lips. "Does that bother you?" he asked between planting soft kisses on her knuckles.

"No," she said, suddenly breathless, "but those kisses do.''

He laughed lazily, gliding his tongue between her fingers. "Good," he drawled, "I've found another weapon.''

She felt herself fill with need as his tongue explored the sensitive areas between her fingers. She felt weak, then giddy as an incredible ache permeated her body, urging her toward Kyle. Every part of her wanted to be near him, wanted to touch his body, explore it, feel everything, do it all.

She took a shaky breath and tried to pull her hand away, but he held it tightly, shaking his head and smiling at her. "No way, Delta. You're not getting away tonight. Tonight, my dear, we've reached the final reckoning.''

Eleven

Expecting Kyle to drive home in record time, Delta was more than a little surprised when they ended up at the airport in Hyannis.

"What's this?" she asked dryly, having recovered her aplomb, "Stopping for a late-night chat with the guys in the bar?"

He just smiled mysteriously, leaned over and kissed her lazily. "You'll see."

"When?" she asked as he got out. She scrambled from the car and found him opening the trunk. "Dropping off a spare tire to be fixed?" she asked acidly, her green eyes sparkling with anger. Of all the lousy ways to start a romantic evening! He'd had her panting, and here he was fooling around in the trunk at a godforsaken airport.

He took two suitcases from the trunk and slammed the lid. "No spare tires, Delta," he said, one corner of his mouth lifted in amusement. "Just a couple of suitcases with only the essentials."

"Essentials for what?" she demanded, growing more frustrated by the moment.

"For a romantic rendezvous," he answered. "What else?"

She simply stared.

He shoved one suitcase under his arm, picked up the other, took her elbow and swept her up in his wake. "I'm talking about the little trip we're going to take."

She skidded to a stop, almost dislodging the suitcases Kyle held so precariously. "Wait just a minute here," she said. "What in blue blazes are you talking about?"

"I'm talking about seduction, Delta," he explained reasonably. "About romance, black lace nightgowns, champagne and roses."

"You're talking nonsense," she said stoutly, folding her arms.

He half shrugged, then turned and walked toward the terminal.

"Wait a minute!" she shouted, running to catch up. "What's going on here, Frederick?" she demanded indignantly. "Have you lost what few marbles you've got?"

He shrugged again, pushed open the door, set the suitcases down and tugged his tie loose. "You ready, Alvin?" he asked a young man who was lounging in a chair watching television.

The young man looked up and grinned. "Sure am, Kyle." His eyes wandered toward Delta and lit up appreciatively. "'Bout time you found a woman with some class," he said, then got up, settled a baseball cap on his curly mop of blond curls and walked out.

"This is enough," Delta said under her breath, her voice vibrating with indignity. "I've had it. Either you stand right here and tell me what the hell is going on or I deck you. What'll it be, Frederick?"

"I made reservations at an inn on Nantucket. Alvin's a pilot. He's flying us there. We'll be met by a limousine and driven to the inn." He nodded toward the suitcases. "I took the liberty of buying you a few sexy little things."

She closed her mouth abruptly, the wind knocked out of her sails. "*Two* suitcases worth of sexy little things?" she finally asked weakly.

"No, honey, only one. The other's mine."

"I see."

"Well?" he asked. "Are you going with me or not?"

"I didn't know I had a choice," she said. "You've been acting like a caveman. For a minute there I thought you'd just grab me by the hair and drag me along."

"Come to think of it, that probably *is* what I'll do if you refuse."

She looked at him in surprise. Here was a man who knew what he wanted and went after it. She found she liked that— especially when *she* was what he wanted.

She yawned elaborately and patted her hair. "Well, seeing as we're here..." she said, managing to sound bored.

He grinned at her, picked up the suitcases and took her arm. "Yawn now, honey," he said, "'cause when we get to that inn, you're not going to have time for sleeping."

"No?" she asked, batting her lashes at him innocently. "What will I have time for? A manicure? A lazy soak in the tub?" She smiled sweetly. "Breakfast in bed?"

"Definitely breakfast in bed," he growled before herding her into the small plane. "And anything else you might have in mind, too."

"Anything?"

He leaned over and kissed her hard. "Anything."

For some reason she suddenly couldn't think of another thing to say.

Nantucket lay in the dark ocean like an ebony jewel encrusted with glittering lights. The small plane swooped down from the black sky, guided by rows of tiny red and blue lights. Its engine coughed and sputtered, then the wheels hit land and the plane bumped to a stop.

"Nine o'clock tomorrow?" Alvin asked when he'd unloaded the suitcases.

"Right," Kyle said, shaking hands with the pilot. "See you then."

A silver limousine was waiting for them, complete with an opened bottle of champagne and two crystal flutes. Delta sat back on the plush velvet seats and touched her glass to Kyle's.

"To us," he said, "and happiness."

"To happiness." She sipped the champagne, but didn't need it. She was already dizzy from everything Kyle had planned. She also had an irresistible urge to be closer to him, but he remained steadfastly on his side of the wide car. Only his eyes caressed her, and strangely, they were even more potent than his touch. She felt warmed by the light she saw in them and filled with delicious expectation. Her body tingled, and she became achingly aware of her body, the way her nylons whispered when she crossed her legs.

The limousine cruised to a stop in front of an impressive brick building on a side street. Lights gleamed cheerfully in the windows, and somewhere in the distance a group of people laughed. The pleasant sound echoed in the silent night as the limousine drove away and Kyle led her up the steps to the front door.

The black-painted door opened onto a wide corridor covered by an ancient Oriental rug. Arrangements of spring flowers, which were reflected in gilt-edged mirrors, sat atop mahogany sideboards that gleamed against the walls. A silver-haired man sat puffing peacefully on a pipe at the main desk. When they appeared, he looked up from his paper and smiled.

"Evening," he said cheerfully. "You must be Mr. and Mrs. Frederick."

"That's right," Kyle said easily, signing the register while Delta felt her face grow pink.

"The suite's ready, Mr. Frederick," the old man said, smiling. "We hope you enjoy it."

"I'm sure we will," Kyle said, then took Delta's elbow as a teenager picked up the luggage and mounted the stairs ahead of them.

"Suite?" Delta whispered as they walked behind the teenager down a long corridor. "Did he say *suite*?"

"Sure did," Kyle said, his eyes gleaming at her.

"For one lousy night you got a *suite*?" she asked hoarsely.

"First of all, my dear, the night will not be lousy," Kyle said dryly. "And second, you deserve it."

That silenced her. She watched quietly as the boy unlocked the door and brought their bags into the next room. As Kyle tipped him, Delta looked around the spacious sitting room. It was graciously elegant, with an Oriental rug on the floor, a white sofa with a butler's tray table stacked with books, magazines and a bowl of fruit in front of a fireplace, two wing chairs upholstered in striped blue silk, and French doors overlooking a small terrace.

"It's beautiful," she said, gazing around the room, "but honestly, Kyle, you didn't have to do this. My place would have been fine."

"I wanted to do this," he said, taking a bottle of champagne from a silver ice bucket and wrapping a towel around it to cushion the removal of the cork. "Why don't you take a bath, if you want, then open the black suitcase and change into something more comfortable. I'll be here when you're ready."

"You won't get ... bored?"

He indicated the stack of books on the coffee table. "I'll have company." His eyes seemed to grow darker. "And waiting always makes the prize that much more rewarding."

She took a shaky breath and turned on her heel, escaping into the sanctuary of the bedroom. She closed the door, then leaned back against it, taking in the king-size four-poster with a white satin canopy and bedspread, the plush forest-green carpeting, the fireplace with marble mantel where a fire crackled cheerfully in the hearth, the love seat upholstered in celadon-striped silk. On a round table next to the bed a dozen red roses stood in a crystal vase.

Slowly she approached the two suitcases and opened the black one. She found a black negligee trimmed in lace, a bottle of perfume, dusting powder and a white silk robe. She picked up the robe and held it to her cheek, then closed her eyes and inhaled deeply. The scent of roses came to her from a sachet Kyle had tucked into the suitcase.

He'd gone to so much trouble, and all for her. She looked around, awed by all that he'd planned to ensure their first night together would be special. She hurried into the bathroom and began running a bath. She was going to go all out, because a night like tonight might never come again.

Delta rubbed the crystal stopper from the perfume bottle over the inside of her wrist, dabbed a spot on the pulse of her throat and behind her ears, then took a deep breath and examined herself in the mirror. Her critical eye could find nothing to fault. True, she wasn't as sleek and lanky as a cover girl, but she was nicely shaped, beautifully scented and lavishly dressed in the sexiest negligee she had ever seen. The front dropped daringly, accentuating her full breasts, and the lace was provocatively sheer. She pulled on the white silk robe and tied the belt, then moved quietly through the darkened bedroom toward the living room.

When she opened the door, she was greeted by the blues playing quietly on the sound system. Kyle was seated on the couch, his jacket off, his tie removed, the first four buttons of his white shirt undone. His shoes were lying on the floor near the couch, and he had rolled up his sleeves to the elbows, exposing the crisp blond hair on his muscular forearms.

Delta felt a delicious spasm curl and uncurl in her midsection, then she closed the door and Kyle looked up, his eyes growing warm as he watched her walk toward him.

"Did I take too long?" she asked softly.

He shook his head, his eyes moving up and down her figure. "No, you're worth waiting for."

She came to a stop in front of him, feeling nervous tremors shake her sensitive body. Slowly he reached out and ran a hand up her arm beneath the sleeve of her robe. He tugged her forward.

"Come here," he murmured, sounding lazy, sleepy and incredibly sexy all at once.

She moved closer, but remained standing. Gently he pressed his head into her abdomen and inhaled deeply. "You smell so good," he murmured, running his hands up the back of her thighs to cup her buttocks.

She felt a flash of heat shoot through her, felt her bones turn to butter, then he parted her robe and pressed soft kisses on her abdomen through the lace of her negligee. Her knees buckled, and she sank onto the couch beside him, her pent-up breath escaping on a soft, wistful sigh.

"You feel so good, Delta," Kyle crooned, kissing her face gently.

Eyes closed, she ran her hands up his broad back. "Mmm, so do you," she said breathlessly.

Kyle ran his hand over her midriff, then down her hip to her thigh. "You're firm," he said against her lips, "but you're soft, too. I like the way your body curves in the right places. Your skin is like velvet under my hands."

She groaned and wrapped her arms around his neck, bending his head toward hers. "Stop talking," she whispered, "and kiss me."

He teased her with his lips, which hovered over hers. Then he brushed his lips softly against hers, his breath sweet, his arms strong around her.

"You're driving me mad," she whispered, running her hands through his hair and bending his head closer to hers, then kissing him deeply, parting her lips to allow her tongue to play over his.

He inhaled sharply and opened his mouth, trapping her tongue against his. She sank against him, loving the feel of his tongue and the way his body was pressed so tightly against hers.

"Do you like the room?" he murmured while nuzzling her ear.

"It's beautiful," she whispered raggedly.

"Do you like your nightgown?"

"Mmm. Do you?"

He groaned and laughed hoarsely. "Yeah," he finally managed. "But then I knew I would—I bought it."

He was nibbling on her ear, sending concentric circles radiating outward from her stomach, increasing in size as they circled, sending pulsing heat to the rest of her body. He bent her back against the couch cushions and pressed kisses into the hollow of her throat while he stroked the hardening blossom of her breast. She moaned softly, holding his head against her throat, inhaling the musky odor of his aftershave. He kissed the valley between her breasts relentlessly while he caressed her aroused nipples. Then he pushed the fragile lace off her shoulders and bared her full breasts, cupping them in his palms and dropping soft kisses on them, kisses that sent her pulse slamming against her skin and made her weak with longing.

She grew restive, found herself wanting more, yet it all felt so good she didn't know what she wanted most. His lips were wonderful, and his hands worked magic on her breasts, but she wanted his touch everywhere, wanted to feel his naked body against hers, to run her hands up and down his muscular back, to feel his skin on hers, unhampered by clothing. And while she thought these things, he nuzzled her nipples with his nose, then laved them with his tongue, sucking first one then the other into his mouth, sending her blood coursing through her veins at rocket speed.

She murmured incoherently and unbuttoned his shirt, then slid her hands inside, reveling in the tactile pleasure of his hair-roughened chest and the smooth skin of his muscular back. He sat back and shucked off his shirt, looking down at her with eyes that had darkened with passion.

"We need more room," he murmured. "What a shame to be hampered by this couch when there's a perfectly respectable king-size bed in the other room."

She smiled lazily, running her hands hypnotically over his chest. "The only trouble is, we have to get from here to there, and I don't feel like moving."

"I think I can remedy that," he said, and gathered her into his arms, picking her up as if she weighed no more than a feather.

She put her arms around his neck and nestled against him, feeling small yet safe, vulnerable yet incredibly sexy. The walk from the living room to the bedroom seemed to take forever, and she was glad, for it seemed a particularly symbolic journey, as if she were discarding an old self and replacing it with a new one. She felt as if this time she would keep her weight off, that Kyle was the man she'd wanted all these years, the one whose absence in her life had led her to overeat to fill the void.

When he placed her against the pillows, she kept her hands linked behind his head and stared up into his eyes, her own eyes darker than normal. "I feel so lucky," she whispered, "as if fate led me to your name in the phone book."

He smiled down at her, then lowered himself beside her and began to stroke her, his large hand moving lovingly from breast to waistline to hip and back again to repeat the cycle. "I feel lucky, too," he murmured, dropping soft kisses on her breasts and midriff, then nuzzling her lace-draped abdomen. "When you opened the door that day, I felt as if someone had kicked me in the solar plexus. You knocked the wind right out of my lungs you were so beautiful."

She frowned, trying to believe him. "Didn't it bother you that I was overweight?"

"Your weight didn't matter. All I had to do was look at you and I fell in love." He searched her eyes. "You can't believe that, can you? You seem to think that men only want women who are skin and bones. You can't seem to grasp that loving someone has nothing to do with how much they weigh or what they look like. It's a matter of the heart, Delta, and of the spirit. Something in you reached out to me and snared me. I love you, Delta."

She closed her eyes, shaking her head back and forth against the pillow. "Don't say that word, Kyle," she pleaded softly. "Let's not even talk about love. Let's just enjoy what we have for tonight, and if it lasts that's wonderful, and if it doesn't—''

"No, Delta," he murmured in a low, passionate voice, "don't even think that way. You're leaving yourself an escape hatch, talking about living only for the moment. I want to live all my life with you, not just tonight."

She looked up at him with eyes that glowed, but she shook her head almost sadly at him. "Oh, Kyle," she breathed, smiling in spite of her fear, "my incurable romantic."

"Is it so romantic to know you love someone?" he asked softly. "Is it foolish to admit how you feel?"

She felt warmth shimmering inside her, as if a low fire burned deep within her, heating her, chasing away all fear. "But you hardly know me," she countered, trying to fight the euphoria that threatened to rise within her with logic. Suddenly her face clouded. "You don't have to tell me you love me," she whispered urgently. "Just make love to me. That's all I ask for now."

"And that's what's been wrong all your life, Delta," he said fervently. "You've never allowed yourself to expect more. You've settled for half a loaf when you deserve three or four whole ones. Demand it now for yourself, Delta. Don't settle for just sex when I'm offering you my love."

His words were lethal, she realized. He was insidious, sneaking past her defenses and insinuating himself into her life. She closed her eyes and drew him down to her, burying her head against his strong shoulder. "Oh, God," she breathed tormentedly. "I love you, too, Kyle. I love you so much."

His arms were strong around her and he was kissing her heatedly, demandingly, his tongue like a hot saber thrust into her mouth again and again, an invasion of her entire body and spirit. He dragged her nightgown off, his hands shaking, his muscles bunching and loosing as he trailed ardent kisses down her hips to her thighs.

He turned her over and kissed the back of her knees, then ran his tongue back and forth over the sensitive skin before

kissing a heated line down the back of her calves to her an-
kles and the soles of her feet. Sensually he flicked his tongue
over and around her toes so that her breathing stabbed at
her lungs and she gasped for breath, clutching at him desperately, feeling as if she were sinking in a deep pool, in-
undated by warm waters of arousal such as she'd never
experienced.

He ran his hand up her leg, between her calves, up her
silken thigh, pausing at the juncture of her legs, tantalizing
her with his caresses.

"Lord, I want you," he growled deep in his throat. "I
want you in every way there is to want a woman. I want to
sink inside you, to bury myself in you so deeply that I'm one
with you, a part of you, indissoluble."

His heated words, spoken in that low voice that trembled
with emotion, acted on her as no physical stroking could
have done. She began to shake, and her body became all
fiery liquid, heated past all reason. Nothing in the world
could have stopped what was to happen—no act of man or
God could have kept her from Kyle's loving embrace. It was
as if somewhere in some gilded ledger her name had been
entered next to his, to live with him forever, possessing each
other, part of each other's life.

She cried his name softly, and he was suddenly with her,
his large body hovering over hers, his lips taking hers in a
demanding kiss while he probed for entrance. She opened
to him willingly, gasping softly as he entered her. Then she
wrapped her arms around his hard body and drew him more
deeply inside, sinking with him into that golden land that
shimmered just out of reach, beckoning, calling them to
glory.

They seemed made for each other. He filled her, sinking
deeper and deeper into her until she cried out incoherently,
her face filled with rapture as she approached fulfillment.

But while she knew it was inevitable, she didn't want it to
end, didn't want to lose this shimmering beauty. It was too
beautiful, too wonderful to have it end.

"Oh, Kyle," she cried softly, "Please don't stop, don't ever stop."

But it did end, in shattering cataclysm, breaking her apart and tearing her world asunder in an explosion so fierce that for a moment she stopped breathing. She stayed there on the mountaintop, suspended for precious moments, then tumbled headlong into fulfillment. They both lay, out of breath, bathed in perspiration, but still joined together as if they would never, after this incredible night, be apart again.

They didn't sleep all night. They made love, they touched, they kissed. They couldn't seem to get enough of each other. It was as if they'd been starved and suddenly found a banquet. They feasted joyously, sampling each other in various ways until at last they fell asleep, still joined, when dawn's first light entered their room.

Once, at eight o'clock, Delta awoke with a start. "Kyle!" she said, shaking him, "Wake up. We have to be at the plane at nine."

He merely smiled drowsily and grunted. "Nine o'clock tonight, Delta, honey," he murmured, pulling her closer and nuzzling her breast. "What do you take me for? A fool?"

"Tonight?" she murmured, sinking fast toward sleep, a satisfied smile curving her lips. She threw her arm over his chest. "You mean we have all day?"

"All day," he said, sliding back toward sleep. "I took this place two nights just so we could have all day here."

Smiling, she was asleep in ten seconds.

He woke her at ten with wanton kisses that trailed hot fire down her body. "I ran a bath for you," he said, resting his cheek on her stomach and eyeing her contentedly. "And while you're in the tub, I'll be shaving. I've ordered breakfast for eleven o'clock, to be delivered here. After that . . ." He shrugged elaborately, his eyes filled with devilment. "Who knows?"

She answered his suggestive grin with a leer of her own and, stretching luxuriously, then wriggled down the bed to join him, kissing his mouth gently as she ran her hand over his chest.

He laughed softly and pulled her on top of him. "The tub's going to fill up and overflow if we don't stop this."

"So?" She started tickling his ear with her tongue.

"You're a brazen hussy," he said, cupping her buttocks and hoisting her atop him.

"Yes," she breathed, sinking onto him. "Yes," she said, "yes, and yes..."

They were thirty minutes late getting to the airport that night, but Alvin was sitting patiently watching television, his baseball cap shoved far back on his head as he munched popcorn and drank a soda. "Thought you two might've forgotten me," he said, grinning amiably as he rose from his chair.

"We wished we could," Kyle admitted, laughing, "but no such luck. Delta's in training, and we have to get back to work."

"You in some sort of competition, ma'am?" Alvin asked.

Delta smiled. "In a matter of speaking, yeah. I'm competing against the clock, you could say. If I don't lose at least four more pounds by Friday, I'm dog meat."

Alvin frowned and scratched his head, then set his baseball cap more firmly on his head. "You sure look fine to me," he said, grinning as his eyes ran appreciatively up and down her figure. "Kyle might know where to take those four pounds off, but I sure as heck can't see a spot I'd want to see any less of."

"Why, Alvin," Delta said, laughing, "you're a charmer."

"Yes, ma'am," he said, grinning back, "and if I were ten years older or you were ten years younger, Kyle here'd have some tough competition."

They flew back through the dark night, and Delta felt as if she'd been dreaming. The time on Nantucket had been unreal, and now they were returning to reality. They left the airport in Hyannis at ten-thirty and drove straight back to her house. She was snuggled up beside Kyle when they rounded the curve and drove into her driveway.

She frowned for a moment, wondering what was wrong. Something wasn't right, but she couldn't figure out exactly what. Then she realized that the lights in the house were on.

"Why are the lights on?" she asked, frowning to herself as she sat up. "I thought I'd turned them all off when we left Saturday night to go out to dinner."

Then she saw the car. "There's someone here!" she said, completely baffled. What was wrong? Had there been a burglary? Were the police here even now, gathering evidence, or trying to find out where she was?

She bolted from the car, hurried up the sidewalk and threw open the front door. But when she immediately recognized the sound of the television, she faltered. Who could be here watching television? She walked toward the family room, puzzled more than afraid.

When she reached the door, she stood and stared. Her mother and her sister were lounging on the couches, painting their toenails as they giggled over a sitcom.

Delta slumped against the door frame. "Oh," she said in relief. "It's only you."

Both women turned and looked at her, startled, then her mother rose and opened her arms. "Delta, honey, you're home!"

"Yes, I'm home," she said. "But what are you two doing here?"

Sheila laughed from the couch, her blond hair spilling over her shoulders, her blue eyes sparkling with amusement. "Isn't that just like Delta?" she asked. "Issuing an invitation, then forgetting all about it." Kyle appeared behind Delta and Sheila slowly sat up, tossing her hair over her shoulder provocatively. "And who have we here, Delta? A little someone you're keeping all to yourself?"

Delta turned cold. She hated that tone of voice, filled with both insinuation and flirtation. Turning, Delta saw Kyle standing just behind her. She felt her heart fall. He was looking at Sheila as if there were no other woman in the world but her. Blinded by sudden tears, Delta rushed down the hall. "I'll be right back," she called out cheerfully. "I'm just going to get our luggage!"

Then she was outside, dragging in great breaths of the cool night air, trying to still the clamor of her heart, biting down on her lip to keep from crying. Dammit, dammit, dammit! Why had Sheila come now of all times? Why did she have the knack of turning up whenever Delta had found someone to love.

Twelve

Delta slammed the lid of the car's trunk, then picked up both suitcases and strode angrily toward the house. When she entered the front door, she could hear Sheila's silvery laughter, punctuated by the low rumble of Kyle's baritone. She paused in the doorway and closed her eyes, feeling a pain dart through her breast.

It couldn't happen again; it just couldn't. It would be too unfair, too unjust.

"Delta?" Her mother's voice interrupted her thoughts.

Delta opened her eyes. "I'm tired," she said hurriedly, forcing an uneasy laugh. "Guess you caught me." She looked curiously at her mother. She was almost an exact duplicate of Sheila—tall, slender, with platinum hair, which was dyed now, and sparkling blue eyes. But where Sheila's face was flawless and free of wrinkle, her mother's was just beginning to show the ravages of time. Crow's-feet radiated from her eyes, and two lines descended from the corners of her mouth, giving her chin the appearance of a puppet's.

But she was still beautiful. If anything, the wrinkles on her face only added to her attractiveness, making it look as if wisdom had been wed to beauty in her face. Startled by this insight, Delta looked even more closely at her mother, as if seeing her for the first time. There was something almost like sadness in her eyes as she looked at her younger daughter, and a strange sweet smile.

"You've lost weight again," her mother said. "You look lovely, Delta. Does that nice Mr. Frederick have anything to do with it?"

Delta dropped the suitcases listlessly. "He's my personal trainer. I'm going to be on Bill Morton's show this Friday. Marcia told me to lose weight or take a hike." She shrugged carelessly, falling into the habits of a lifetime more easily than she could have imagined possible. It had always been this way between her and her mother—her mother's seemingly interested questions, and Delta's pretended indifference.

"Why, Delta!" her mother enthused softly, "I think that's wonderful! You're really going to be on Bill Morton's show?"

Delta eyed her mother curiously. Did that make a difference to her mother? Would this recognition from the world finally win her mother's love? Delta felt her heart drop. She didn't want to have to *win* her mother's love; she wanted it automatically, unconditionally, without having to earn it. Wasn't that what love was all about? Wasn't it a gift, given freely, without having to be earned?

Delta picked up the suitcases tiredly. "Yeah," she said, "I'm really going to be on *Mornings with Morton*." She started for the stairs, but her mother put out a hand and touched her arm softly.

"I'm proud of you, Delta," she said quietly.

Delta shrugged. "It's no big deal," she said offhandedly. "My book's number one on the bestseller list," she added, as if heaping on the accolades would earn her even more love. "I guess my publishers decided to capitalize on it."

She was halfway up the stairs when her mother called to her. "Delta?"

She stopped and looked back. "Yes?"

Her mother stood at the bottom of the steps, looking very old and worried. "You don't seem happy," she said, sounding confused.

Delta shrugged. "Should I be?"

Her mother's frown deepened. "Well, I...I guess *I* would be if I'd accomplished all you have."

"But that's just it, Mother," Delta said. "You never had to accomplish anything in life to get what you wanted most. It just came to you, heaped on silver platters. You and Sheila. Two peas in a pod—" She stopped then, horrified at the expression on her mother's face. It was like looking into a mirror—she saw herself.

For a moment she just stood on the steps and stared, so confused, so muddled and mixed up that she didn't know what to do. She almost went to her mother, for she had a sudden urge to hold and shelter her, to keep her mother from all pain, but years of conditioning held her back. Instead, she simply stared, perplexed, then she turned suddenly and darted up the stairs. She was almost to her bedroom when she heard Sheila's laughter ring out, followed by Kyle's.

She came to a stop. Suddenly she felt old herself, old and very tired. She felt as if she were being sucked back into the past, trapped by all the pain and misunderstanding, by the inability to communicate, by the divisions that kept mother and daughter apart, and divided sister from sister. She wished she could walk out of the house into the night and never stop walking. She wanted clear, cold air, air so pure that it would make her lungs hurt, air that purified her, that burned the pain out of her, that set her free.

Tiredly she walked down the corridor. She left Kyle's suitcase in his room, refusing to stop to look around. She wasn't going to allow herself to get sentimental. She wasn't going to feel anything at all. She was going to laugh and tell jokes and the hell with everyone—her mother and her sister and, most of all, Kyle Frederick.

She unpacked the small black suitcase unemotionally, dropping the black lace nightgown, the white robe, the perfume, the dusting powder and the sachet into the wastebasket, then slammed the lid on the suitcase and kicked it across the room.

Who was she kidding? She was so angry she was shaking, and she was overwhelmingly hungry. Ravenously she looked around the bedroom, knowing it was useless. Her private stock of chocolates had long ago been depleted— Kyle had seen to that. She was living in a home without food, and for Delta, that was like trying to live without oxygen.

She began to pace the room, haunted by visions of Carnaby Chocolate Creams, of doughnuts and pastries and pies, of mounds of ice cream topped with whipped cream and hot fudge. She envisioned masses of potato chips, cookies, cakes. She saw acres of frosting, miles of fudge, billions of brownies. They shimmered in the air before her until she could almost reach out and taste them.

She began to shake even harder, and her pacing increased until finally she was pulling open drawers and upending boxes in a frantic attempt to find what she knew wasn't there. But still she searched, panic-stricken. It was as if she were a junkie who might die if she didn't get food right away. The problem was, no one understood. No one realized what it was like, this ceaseless, burning hunger, this need to chew and swallow and savor the flavors of the forbidden foods of life.

She closed her eyes and saw it—shimmering just out of reach, piles and piles of it, glorious, fulfilling, the epitome of happiness. If she just concentrated hard enough, if she got rid of all distractions, she could reach out and touch it and then everything would be all right. Yes, like this—

"Delta."

Her eyes flew open. She saw Kyle standing in the doorway, watching her with concerned eyes. Guiltily she snapped her hand back, feeling as vulnerable as she'd ever felt in her life.

"What do you want?" Her voice shook as she spoke, and she slowly retreated from him.

He advanced as slowly, pausing only long enough to close the door behind him. "Are you all right?" he asked quietly. "You look upset."

"I'm fine."

"Are you?"

"Of course. Why wouldn't I be?"

"You're not upset that your mother and sister are here?"

"Why should I be? It's typical of them to show up uninvited and unannounced."

"Why are you shaking?"

She put both hands behind her back and clasped them tightly. "I'm not shaking."

"Are you hungry? We didn't have much to eat today after breakfast." He cocked his head to the side. "We were rather busy if you remember."

She felt a spasm of awareness flash through her, and suddenly she was confused. What was she really hungry for—food or Kyle's lovemaking? Suddenly, from the hallway, she heard Sheila's voice.

"Delta? Delta, honey? Which room should I sleep in?"

Delta looked at Kyle, then her eyes flickered to the door. She really should respond. She should go to Sheila and help her get settled.

Kyle advanced on Delta. "Maybe you're not hungry at all," he said in a low, hypnotic voice. "Maybe you want something else besides food."

She looked uneasily at the door behind him. "I . . . I have to go to Sheila."

"Why? She can find her own way around. She got herself in here easily enough."

Delta looked back at Kyle sharply. What was he saying? Did he want to be with *her* and not her beautiful sister? She hesitated, then darted forward, lunging toward the door, but Kyle was there before her, heading her off. Effortlessly he reached out and turned the lock. It snapped loudly in the quiet room. Then he turned off the light, plunging the room into darkness.

"Delta?" Sheila's voice sounded querulous and petulant. "Delta, dammit, I know you're in there!"

Delta's breasts rose and fell in violent rhythm. She couldn't respond to her sister's call. She could only stand and stare at Kyle, feeling everything inside her build to the screaming point. She should go to Sheila. It was her duty.

"Aren't you hungry, Delta?" Kyle asked softly.

She stared at him, feeling suddenly cold, filled with ruthless anger. Damn him, he was teasing her. He knew exactly what he was doing to her and she wouldn't let him. She lunged for the door, but he caught her, pulling her against his strong chest and burying his head in the curve of her neck, whispering into her ear. "Are you hungry, Delta?"

She tried to fight the awareness that coursed through her, but she couldn't. Suddenly she was flooded with sensations, bombarded by a need so huge she felt overwhelmed by it. She struggled soundlessly to free herself from Kyle's arms, but he wouldn't release her. Instead, he inexorably maneuvered her toward the bed and repeated the question. "Are you hungry, Delta?"

She struggled silently, hitting at him with ineffectual fists, shaking her head back and forth, biting her lips to keep from crying out.

He lifted her in his arms and turned around with her, turning and turning in a dizzying circle, then he placed her on the bed, following her down, trapping her beneath his large body. "Tell me what you want, Delta," he grated hoarsely, stinging her with hot kisses on her throat, her neck, her ears, her mouth.

"We *can't*," Delta whispered frantically. "They're out there!"

"We can," he said, beginning to unbutton her blouse, letting his lips sear her skin with fiery kisses.

She was being tugged underneath deep waters, waters so black she couldn't see, but she couldn't resist their hypnotic pull. She sank into them, tearing at the buttons on Kyle's shirt with trembling fingers, then finding his naked chest with her lips and hands, exploring, kissing, caressing, ravenous with need.

"Hurry," she whispered, hiking up her hips to remove her slacks and panties.

"Delta!" Sheila called from far down the hall. "Where *are* you?"

Delta laughed softly and tugged at the zipper on Kyle's trousers, helping him remove them.

They fell into glorious partnership. He plunged into her and she lifted her hips to him, welcoming his dark invasion, glorying in it. She was filled by his hardness, held by his strong arms, cradled beneath his hard body.

"Oh, yes," she whispered raggedly. She was so hungry, and he was filling her. She was ravenous, and he was there, inside her, chasing away the void.

They seemed locked in mortal combat. The more she asked, the more he gave. She sank her fingernails into his back and urged him on with inchoate whimpers, and he responded, his thrusts as hungry as her need. On Nantucket they had made love. Now they simply mated. It was instinctive and raw, and their climax was more a battle cry than a cry of satisfaction.

At the end she lay beneath him, bathed in perspiration, panting, holding on to him, her eyes squeezed fiercely shut.

"Are you still hungry?" he asked.

She took an unsteady breath. "No."

He began to stroke her skin, still bathed with the sheen of sweat. "This was what you've wanted all along," he said, "not food at all. It's never been food. It's always been this."

She opened her eyes and lay staring up at the ceiling where strips of light lay across its surface, reflecting from the outdoor lighting she'd left on. "How did you know I wanted food?" she finally asked.

"I know you."

"How?"

He shrugged. "It's instinctive, I think. I just know you."

She began to rub his bare back. "I love you," she said.

He began to kiss her lazily. "And I love you. Do you want to make love again?"

She sighed, feeling incredibly relaxed. "So soon?"

"Amazingly enough," he said, laughing softly, "I could."

"You *are* something," she said admiringly.

"So are you."

She turned her head and looked into his eyes. She wanted to ask him about Sheila, but she was afraid to.

"What?" he asked.

She shook her head. "Nothing."

"It was something," he insisted. "What was it you wanted to say?"

She lay silently, then kissed him. "I want to make love again," she said. "That's what I wanted to say."

He looked at her a long moment, then entered her as though he belonged there. "Like this?"

She began to shudder. "Yes," she said, her voice breaking as her body reacted to his presence inside her. "Yes," she whispered again. "Yes."

This time was slower, more loving, and the climax almost gentle. They held each other, sighing, then fell asleep. In the night, Delta woke up and looked at Kyle. He slept peacefully, his face illuminated by the dim light that crept into the darkened room from outside.

"I love you," she whispered, suddenly feeling afraid. She moved closer to him and put her arms across his chest. In his sleep, he grunted and stroked her arm, then relaxed again into slumber. She lay awake a long time, holding him, wondering why Sheila and her mother had come, feeling a small, hard knot of doubt insinuate itself inside her.

Something wasn't right. She knew it. If her mother and Sheila were here, something terrible was going to happen.

"Come on, Delta," Kyle urged cheerfully the next morning while they jogged, "you're not keeping up. Is something on your mind?"

"What?" Delta looked at Kyle as if he were a complete stranger.

He smiled easily. "Don't tell me a weekend in bed with me has this kind of effect on you."

She threw him a wry look. "Ha! It's my sister and mother I'm thinking about, not you."

"You're just saying that for my ego," Kyle teased.

Delta frowned, ignoring him completely. "Sheila said something about having been invited, but I didn't invite her and Mother here."

Kyle jogged with his eyes straight ahead. "No?"

"No. They just decided to show up and make me miserable."

"You sure have a high opinion of your family."

Delta looked shamefaced. "Oh, Kyle, I know how it sounds, but the fact is that Sheila and I have had a terrible case of sibling rivalry ever since my mother brought me home from the hospital. And Mother . . ."

"What about her?"

Delta shrugged, having slowed to a walk. "She's just always favored Sheila."

"Is that true, or do you just feel that way?"

"It's true!" Delta said heatedly. "Sheila always brought home boyfriends and beauty pageant titles, and she was homecoming queen at college three years in a row, and—" Delta sighed. "Oh, well, it's clear from just looking at her that she's a knockout."

"Well, you're right about one thing," Kyle admitted. "She is beautiful."

Delta stiffened. "Oh? You think she's pretty?"

"No, I think she's beautiful. Pretty doesn't do her justice."

Delta raised her chin, her face suddenly stony. "Well, it looks as if my sister has conquered another suitor of mine."

"Hey, Delta," Kyle teased, "I just said she was beautiful. I didn't say I wanted to run off with her."

"No, but given the chance, you would," Delta said knowingly. "You're just like every other man on the face of the earth. Once a male sees Sheila, I can just kiss him goodbye.''

"Jog, Delta," Kyle ordered crisply. "Forget your sister. You've got four days until *Mornings with Morton*. Let's not blow it now.''

"No, you wouldn't want to fail, would you, Kyle?" Delta asked coolly. "But I'm sure you certainly didn't count on Sheila showing up.''

Kyle seemed about to reply, then he shrugged and sprinted on ahead. "I'll meet you back at the house, Delta," he yelled back over his shoulder. "We've got floor exercises to do to make up for slacking off yesterday.''

"Oh?" she called out sweetly. "I thought I got more than enough exercise, Mr. Frederick. You sure saw to that.''

He turned and grinned at her, then waved and sprinted even farther ahead. "See you back at the house.''

"Try to stay away from Sheila," Delta shouted sweetly. "She'll have you eating out of her hand.''

"If I got fat, I could go on one of your diets," he yelled back.

"If you got fat, it would probably only be in your head," she shouted, "and none of my diets work on fatheads.''

He turned and jogged backward, a wide grin splitting his face. "Keep it up, Delta. As long as your tongue is still sharp, I know you're in fighting form.''

"Just remember that, Frederick," she shouted. "You're my personal trainer, not Sheila's. If she asks for suggestions for what to do for her figure, ignore her until after Friday.''

"But, Delta," he wailed petulantly, in perfect imitation of Sheila, "that's not fair. I'd only be doing my job.''

"Not on my time, buster," she said, running harder until she caught up with him. "Keep your mind on business and concentrate on me. Let Sheila cool her heels until after I make myself famous Friday.''

"You mean you're only interested in me for business reasons?" Kyle asked, feigning hurt. "And here I thought you went with me to Nantucket because you were in love with me."

"I went with you to Nantucket because you left me no alternative." She eyed him sardonically. "And isn't it sad that your timing was so bad? I bet if you'd known Sheila was coming, you'd never have made reservations at an inn for the weekend."

Kyle turned his head and observed her with strangely knowing eyes. "Oh?" he asked, then began to chuckle. "Come on, Delta, let's run the next mile flat out."

With that, he was gone, accelerating with the ease of an eight-cylinder automobile. Delta sighed and stepped up her pace a little, but he was far ahead of her, running easily. She sighed to herself, wondering if she could keep up the cheerful irony much longer. Then she shrugged. She had to. Until Friday she would just have to put up with Sheila's presence and pretend that Kyle's interest in her sister didn't bother her in the least.

By the time Delta got back to the house, Kyle was ending his cool-down exercises and Sheila was oohing and aahing over him while strutting around in a skimpy white tennis dress. Delta tamped down rising panic and watched her sardonically.

"Do you play tennis, Kyle?" Sheila asked, batting her lashes and flipping her platinum hair coquettishly over her shoulder.

"No, Sheila," Kyle said, smiling easily, "that's one sport I never took up."

"Oh, darn!" Sheila said, pouting. "And I so wanted to play with you!"

"I'll bet," Delta said darkly under her breath.

"Did you say something, Delta?" Sheila asked, smiling brightly at her sister who was halfway through her own cool-down exercises.

"Not a thing," Delta answered airily. "Why don't you ask Mother to play?"

"Oh, Mother!" Sheila said dismissively. "She's such a spoilsport. She said she wanted to walk the beach and look for shells." Sheila rolled her eyes. "Honestly, did you ever hear of anything more *boring*?"

"I like looking for shells," Kyle commented.

"*Do* you?" Sheila looked him over, as if seeing everything in a new light. "Well, maybe it wouldn't be too boring if a good-looking man like you were along."

"Yeah, but I doubt you'd be looking for shells very long," Delta said under her breath. "You'd have other kinds of booty on your mind."

"What, Delta?" Sheila asked, frowning at her.

"I didn't say anything," Delta said cheerfully, straightening to smile brightly at her sister. "Something wrong with your ears?"

Kyle glanced from Delta to Sheila, then gave Delta a knowing look. "I'll be inside, Delta. We need to work on some abdominal curls."

"Be right there," Delta said, watching as he walked into the house.

Sheila turned to Delta when he was gone. "You're sleeping with him, aren't you?" she asked archly.

"I don't think that's really any of your business."

"No?" Sheila asked, smiling coyly. "Then why did he call me up and specifically ask me to come for a visit?"

Delta looked up slowly from tying her shoelaces. "What did you say?"

"You heard me," Sheila said, throwing Delta a triumphant smile. "He said he'd heard so much about me from you he just had to meet me. He didn't ask Mother to come, he asked *me*. Just *me*, Delta. So you may be sleeping with him now, but you won't be much longer." With that, Sheila turned and strolled toward the house, her hips swaying provocatively as she swung her tennis racket and hummed a few notes from the theme from *Dragnet*. "Dum-de-dum-dum. Dum-de-dum-dum. *Dum*!"

Thirteen

————

Delta crammed a Carnaby Chocolate Cream into her mouth, her temper at full boil. "Of all the lowdown, conniving, rotten things to do," she sputtered, swallowing the candy, popping another into her mouth and chewing frantically. "He's no better than a Don Juan, a Casanova!" She picked up two more candies and crammed them into her mouth one after the other, not even pausing to savor them.

She sat in her car in the parking lot behind the Kandy Kupboard in Hyannis, decimating a pound of Carnaby Chocolate Creams while spouting a litany of grudges against Kyle. "He's been playing a game all along!" she said out loud, licking her fingers and reaching for another candy. "He seduced me to get me to lose weight. Well, I'll show him! I'll gain so much weight in four days, I'll make the *Guinness Book of World Records*!"

She closed her eyes and forced herself to swallow another candy. She felt slightly queasy, but that was just the price she would have to pay. She would show the rotten no-good cad what she thought of him and his words of love!

She looked uneasily at the half-eaten box of candy and suddenly wished for a cool glass of water. She frowned. What was wrong with her? In the past she'd always been able to eat a pound of Carnaby Chocolate Creams without stopping. But after two and a half weeks of fish and fresh vegetables, the candy didn't taste right. Suddenly it tasted cloyingly sweet, and she pushed the box away and sat staring mulishly out the window.

No matter. Pretty soon she would finish this box and begin on the next. By the time she reached home, she would have polished off two pounds of candy and would be well into the brownies she'd bought at the bakery. After that, there were éclairs and an entire chocolate cake, and two dozen doughnuts. Later she would buy a large pizza and finish it off with a six-pack of beer. Then she would start on her midnight snacks.

She groaned and rested her forehead on the steering wheel. Suddenly she wasn't feeling well. She rolled down the window and inhaled deeply, hoping the salt-tinged fresh air would calm her queasy stomach, but nothing seemed to work. Slowly she rolled up the window, then opened the door and got out, locking the car behind her. She needed a good long walk to clear her head and prepare herself for the ordeal that lay ahead.

That stopped her. Ordeal? Since when was overeating an ordeal? For years it had been her only solace, her sole means of comforting herself. Now, after only two and a half weeks on Kyle's weight-loss campaign, she rebelled against the idea of cramming food in and longed instead for a bracing walk.

Slowly she began to chuckle. The laugh was on her. Kyle had somehow programmed her to reject all that was bad for her and want everything that was healthy. She took a deep breath and looked around. Many of the shops were still closed for the winter, but a few shoppers still strolled the street. Cape Cod had become a year-round haven for senior citizens who retired here in droves, and many people came for vacations in the winter and spring to escape the summer crowds.

She decided to walk toward the harbor and set off at a stiff pace, her head up, her shoulders thrown back, her stride athletic and healthy. She inhaled deeply and tried not to think about Kyle's duplicity, but it haunted her. By the time she reached the harbor, she realized that she would have to confront Kyle rather than pay him back with weight gain. That would only do her harm; it wouldn't faze him in the least.

But she'd never been very good at confronting people. Confrontations were messy, after all. They involved getting angry, and Delta had never been able to handle her anger. When she got angry, she ate. But suddenly, eating didn't seem as appetizing, and she realized she needed a whole new approach. Apparently, all her life, at least ever since bringing Jack Peterson home, she'd been handling it counter-productively, hurting herself by overeating.

She sighed and sat down on the pier, letting her legs dangle as she watched the sea gulls swoop and squawk overhead. She should have brought the rest of the goodies she had stockpiled in her car. The sea gulls would have a field day with them. As it was, she decided she would stop at a nursing home and leave the sweets for the inhabitants. That way, she wouldn't have wasted her money.

She got up tiredly and brushed off her seat, then set off for her car, walking briskly but feeling anything but perky. Now that she had admitted her anger, she felt as if a huge stone were sitting on her chest. This wasn't anger anymore, she realized, it was just plain pain. She'd trusted Kyle, had allowed herself to believe him, had even fallen in love with him.

A searing ache arced through her, and tears pricked at her eyelids, but she batted them away and took a deep breath, trying to dislodge the pain. But it persisted, making her feel as if she wanted to cry. Would her entire life be like this? Was she doomed to fall in love with men, only to get fat and chase them away, or have them fall for Sheila?

She arrived at her car and stood looking through the window at the packages that sat on the seat. The half-eaten box of Carnaby Chocolate Creams looked up at her reproachfully. Slowly she unlocked the door and got in, carefully replacing the lid and putting the box back in the sack with the other pound.

She left the candies and cakes at the front desk of the nursing home, then drove home, her hands trembling at the thought of what awaited her. For a minute she wished she hadn't given away all that food. She needed it now, needed the nourishment it could provide. Then she remembered how the chocolate she had eaten earlier had made her feel.

But something was bothering her, niggling far back in her consciousness, trying to force its way out. She found herself remembering last night, and the way Kyle had followed her to her room, as if reading her mind and knowing she would be looking for food. But he had instinctively known it wasn't food she needed at all, and he'd graphically shown her what it was she really craved—love.

Then what was bothering her became crystal clear. Sheila had told her that Kyle had called her and invited just her to come visit. So why had her mother also come? Sheila had also said that Kyle had told her he wanted to meet her because he'd heard so much about her from Delta. But Kyle had told Delta more than once that he loved her. Maybe she should give him the benefit of the doubt. Maybe Sheila was just trying to scare her away.

She frowned. Everything between her and Sheila had been a battle all their lives, and Sheila had always won. Or maybe Delta had just let her. When Jack Peterson fell for Sheila, Delta had retreated to her room to mope and begin the seemingly endless cycle of binging on food. Now it hit her that if she wanted Kyle's love she would have to fight for it.

She slowed the car and came to a halt at a dangerous curve overlooking the harbor. Sick with fear, she stared at the water unseeingly. She didn't know how to fight for a man, didn't know the first thing about defending what was rightly hers. Stunned, she stared straight ahead, hearing her own thoughts with vivid clarity. *What was rightly hers.* Suddenly she knew something monumental had happened in her life—she felt *entitled* to happiness and love. Never before had she felt she truly deserved love, so she'd sat back and let Sheila steal her boyfriend, and she'd later sabotaged her own chances at happiness by gaining weight and chasing away any man who might fall for her.

A car came hurtling around the curve, and the driver hit his brakes and horn at the same time, before swerving around her while shaking his fist and shouting a vivid curse. Shaking, Delta put the car into gear and guided it into the gravel turnaround that allowed sightseers to park safely and gaze at the harbor. She didn't know what had shaken her up more—her realization of how she had changed or the near miss with the other car.

She rested her forehead against the steering wheel and realized that she'd literally and figuratively been parked at a dangerous place in her life, but somehow she'd gotten through the danger. That didn't make returning home to a confrontation any easier, of course. If anything, it made it harder. Now, when she needed the comfort of food, she didn't have it any longer. She was without props, alone, more vulnerable than she'd ever been in her life.

She groaned and gnawed on her lip, then realized what she was doing and laughed tiredly. She would probably always have this oral fixation—a need to chew on something in moments of stress. She hoped she would learn to chew on sugarless gum, and not take her frustrations and fears out on calorie-laden food.

Still shaking, she put the car into gear and looked both ways before pulling out onto the road. She drove with extra caution, as if this new knowledge about herself were as dangerous as the car at the curve had been. Wouldn't it be a good joke on her if she had an accident now, just when she'd learned so much? She had this terrible fear that she would never make it home, that somehow she would be cheated out of all the happiness she'd only now come to realize she deserved.

That was superstition, of course, but real just the same, so that by the time she guided her car into her driveway, she was shaking even harder than she had been when she'd started out. She cut the engine and then just sat there, taking deep breaths and trying to chase the butterflies from her stomach. If only she hadn't eaten those Carnaby Chocolate Creams.

At that thought, she began to chuckle. Slowly her laughter escalated until she was sitting in her car collapsed with hilarity, holding her stomach while tears ran down her face and she howled at the situation.

Wasn't life ridiculous? She'd always had a sense of humor to fall back on, and luckily it was still with her. It was the only thing she had now—that and the promise of Kyle, if she played her cards right and didn't chase him away.

That possibility sobered her instantly. With trembling fingers she wiped away the traces of tears and then examined her face in the mirror. She looked a little ragged, but then what did you expect when a person had just been through life-challenging trauma?

Taking a deep, bracing breath, she straightened her shoulders and got out of the car. Immediately she felt her knees begin to buckle, so she put a hand out to steady herself against the car.

"Courage," she said out loud to herself, then patted the car's fender and headed for the house.

She found Sheila falling all over Kyle in the family room. Her half sister was dressed in a leotard that left little to the imagination. Delta ran a critical eye over Sheila and saw to her amazement that Sheila, though outwardly trim, looked a little lumpy in the figure-hugging leotard. Feeling an infusion of confidence from this unexpected bonus, Delta entered the room.

"Taking some tips from Kyle, are you, Sheila?" she asked.

Startled, Sheila turned and stared, then shrugged nonchalantly. She ran a languid hand down his brawny arm and smiled intimately at him. "I never pass up the opportunity to spend time with a good-looking man. You know that, Delta."

"I sure do," Delta said clearly. "You started with Jack Peterson, and it looks as if you haven't stopped yet."

Sheila looked around, clearly startled at Delta's mood. Kyle looked up slowly, a strange light in his clear blue eyes. One corner of his mouth twitched, but no other expression crossed his face. He looked remote and detached, as if this had nothing to do with him.

"I wasn't aware Kyle was your boyfriend, Delta," Sheila taunted. "I thought he was just your personal trainer."

"That's not true and you know it," Delta answered. "You know darned well Kyle and I—" She broke off. She'd been about to say they were sleeping together, but that sounded wrong. She felt her face turn pink. "I care for Kyle," she said quietly. "I don't like it when you flirt with the men I care for, Sheila. There are enough men in the world for you. You don't have to pick on mine."

"Yours?" Sheila said, arching a fine brow. "My, how possessive we sound. Does Kyle know he's not only your personal trainer, but your personal property as well? I always thought men didn't like possessive women, but maybe I was wrong."

Delta began to feel nervous. Kyle wasn't saying anything, and she was afraid Sheila was right. Men *didn't* like possessive women. She darted a wary glance at Kyle but could detect nothing from his face. Nervously she licked her lips and looked away, then squared her shoulders. Dammit, she wasn't going to let Sheila get to her by playing on her fears.

"I'm not being possessive," she said quietly. "I'm just telling you how I feel. I care for Kyle, and he knows I do. I just wish you'd stop flirting with him, because it hurts me when you flirt with my boyfriends."

"Why?" Sheila taunted. "Because you know you can't compete?"

Delta took an unsteady breath. She felt cornered. She wanted to turn and run away, but should she admit it? She stared at her beautiful half sister and remembered all the years of pain she had harbored, but suddenly it didn't seem to matter. That was all in the past, and this was now. She remembered her insight from a week or so ago that perhaps Sheila was unhappy for some reason. She decided to reach out to her, to see if she could make some sort of connection for the first time in their lives.

"Sheila," she said softly, "I could never compete with you. You're beautiful. Why, I remember when we were growing up, I'd stand at the door to your bedroom and peer in at you through the crack, and I'd wish I could look just like you, and *be* like you. But I never could. I had this terrible curly hair and a lumpy little body and *green* eyes and—"

"Green eyes are beautiful," Sheila said quietly. "I always wished I had green eyes."

Delta stared at her half sister. "You did?"

Sheila nodded soberly. "I did. I envied your sense of humor, too. You always made people laugh. All I ever did was look pretty, but you glowed when you laughed, and everyone loved you."

"Loved *me*?" Delta squeaked. "That's not true! They loved *you*?"

"Oh, Delta," Sheila said sadly, "you're so stupid sometimes. Do you think love that's based on how a person looks is what really matters? Don't you know that love for what the person is inside is all that counts?"

Delta stared, finally beginning to see. Her efforts had paid off far more than she could have expected. She suddenly didn't know what to say, didn't know how to act. There was too much to take in, and she needed time to digest it all. Awkwardly she looked away and found that her mother was standing in the doorway, listening to them.

"Sheila's right, Delta," her mother said, smiling sadly. "It took me a long time to learn that, and I guess I learned it too late. I'm glad Sheila and you are learning while you're still young enough to profit from it."

"So what do you think of your two daughters now, Mother?" Sheila asked with a stiff laugh. "We're pretty screwed up, eh?"

"I've always loved you both," Delta's mother said, smiling. "And I'm proud of you both, in different ways."

"Well, that's a lovely speech," Sheila said ironically, once again safe behind her facade, "but I'm off. Delta's just laid into me about trying to steal her boyfriend, so I don't feel too welcome."

"Don't leave, Sheila," Delta said suddenly, then swallowed uneasily. She had to carry this thing to its logical end, and that meant confronting Kyle also about his part in this whole matter. It would be best if Sheila stayed to listen and perhaps participate. Secrets were unhealthy, in families or between lovers.

Sheila rolled her eyes. "First she tells me to scram, then she tells me to stick around. Which will it be, Delta? Amscray or stay?"

"Stay," Delta said, her voice suddenly shaking. If it had been bad confronting Sheila, it was ten times worse confronting Kyle, especially with an audience. She took a deep breath and started to speak, only to stop and muddle over her words. She started to speak again, only to stop again.

Sheila sighed loudly and folded her arms. "You going to talk, or are we going to just stand around and watch you take deep breaths?"

"I'm going to talk," Delta said with formal politeness. "K-Kyle," she stammered, squaring her shoulders and lifting her chin resolutely, "Sheila told me you're the one who called her and invited her to come for a visit."

"That's right," he said easily. "I did."

Taken aback by his outright admission, Delta simply stared. She wanted to hit the guy! She wanted to scream and shout invective and claw out his eyes! Instead, she lifted her hands in question. *"Why?"*

"Because of Jack Peterson," he said simply.

"Jack Peterson," Delta repeated dumbly.

"Because that's when you began overeating, and I thought it might have something to do with your relationship with your half sister, so I decided it might be a good idea for you to clear the air a little."

Delta felt two red patches glowing on her cheeks. She lifted her chin even higher and folded her arms. "You did, did you?" she said tightly. "Quite the little psychologist, aren't you?"

"It was presumptuous of me, I'll admit, but I think it worked."

"Oh, you're so smart," Delta said, her green eyes flashing dangerously. "You just make my little ol' head swim with admiration, Kyle Frederick."

"It sounds to me like you're angry," Kyle said, tilting his head consideringly and folding his own arms.

Delta nodded tightly. "You might say that," she snapped.

"No need for us to stay around, Mother," Sheila said, pushing away from the wall languidly. "Let the two love-birds fight it out with each other."

"You may as well stay," Kyle said. "You've heard practically everything, why not hear it all." He faced Delta and said, "You've got a right to be angry, I suppose. I set this situation up. I wanted to see what would happen. So far, I think you've come up all aces."

"What's that supposed to mean?" Delta snapped.

"You faced Sheila. You didn't let her just walk in and work her wiles on me. You stood and fought, and I'm proud of you."

Delta had to look away. He was getting to her, and she didn't want him to. Not yet. She wanted to savor her anger a little longer. All her life she'd sublimated it into hunger. Now she was reveling in its power.

"That still didn't give you the right to pull a trick like this," she said quietly. "I haven't forgiven you, so don't think this is settled between us."

"Okay," Kyle said. "I think my work's about done anyway. I'll move out right now. I think you can manage on your own from now on."

Delta felt a sudden shaft of anxiety dart through her, but she refused to give in to it. She clamped her mouth shut, kept her arms folded and refused to ask him to stay, even though she wanted to more than anything on earth.

Sheila walked out, followed by Kyle, but Delta's mother stayed. "Well," she said lightly, "looks like you've done some major housecleaning, Delta."

Delta nodded glumly. Now that Kyle was gone, she didn't have to pretend any longer. She slumped into a chair and stared into space. "Now it's probably all over between us, just when I thought I'd finally wised up."

"I doubt it's over between you," her mother said fondly. "You two will patch things up."

"That's easy for *you* to say," Delta accused. "You've had good-looking men eating out of your hand since you were ten, but Kyle's my first real lover. I mean, there were a couple of others, but they didn't count. They were practice, I guess."

"And Kyle counts?" her mother asked softly.

"Does he ever," Delta said soulfully.

Her mother patted her hand. "Then things will work out. You just have to believe, Delta."

"But I've never been good at believing," Delta said. "I've always been too afraid to believe in anything but food."

"And Kyle helped change that, didn't he?"

"Yes..." Delta sighed wistfully. "He showed me that food was a poor substitute for love."

It was Delta's mother's turn to sigh. "I have a hunch my daughter's going to be slender from now on. So cheer up! The sun's out. You're thin again, and on Friday you'll be on national television hawking your bestselling book. What else do you need?"

"Kyle."

"Then go after him."

"I can't."

"You can't?" her mother asked, sounding incredulous. "Of course you can! Didn't you just fight Sheila for him?"

"Yes, but that was different. That was because I had to."

"And you don't have to go after Kyle? You can afford to just let the man you love slip through your fingers?"

"Mother, I'm not like you," Delta snapped. "I can't just run after any man who crosses my path and snare him." She put a hand to her mouth in horror. "Oh, Mama, I'm sorry," she whispered. "I didn't mean it that way. That sounded so—" She trailed off, ashamed of herself.

"Of course you meant it," her mother said practically. "And why shouldn't you? That's probably what it looked like to you all those years." She sighed wistfully. "After your father died, I didn't think I'd ever fall in love again, but I tried. Oh, boy, how I tried! I married William Sargeant and Clarence Kelly and Howard Enderman and..." She screwed up her face. "Let's see, who came after Howard? Oh, yes! Bill!" She laughed softly. "Well, Bill was pretty special, I'll have to admit. We lasted almost five years."

Delta stared at her mother. "How do you laugh about it?" she asked suddenly. "It's like it's all a joke."

"You ever wonder where you get your sense of humor, Delta?" her mother asked. "You get it from me. I laugh because if I don't, I'll cry. That's why I understand you so well. It's why you've always been so special to me."

"*I've* been special?" Delta cried. "Oh, Mother, admit it. Sheila's always been the apple of your eye. You didn't even care what my name was. You let me become Delta without batting an eyelash, when you named me Della."

"I *liked* Delta," her mother said. "It fit you. And I love you both, but you've always been very special to me, Delta. I've never admitted that to anyone. I felt guilty about it, so I bent over backward trying not to show favoritism." She picked a piece of lint off her immaculate pink linen dress. "I guess maybe I went overboard. But you see, Delta, your father was the love of my life, and when he died, I wanted to die; but I didn't, because I had two babies, and one of them was his."

Her mother turned loving eyes to Delta. "You were a part of him, Delta, and I treasured you. I still do, I was just afraid to show it. And I ran away, Delta. I ran away from my terrible unhappiness, trying to find another man to make me as happy as your father had, but I couldn't. I went about it all wrong." She shook her head. "I should have dealt with the pain instead of trying to ignore it and hope it would go away. Pain never goes away, Delta. It stays hidden, out of sight, but it does its damage anyway.''

Delta felt tears well up in her eyes, and this time she didn't try to stop them. Suddenly she was hurrying across the room with her arms outstretched. She flung them around her mother, holding her while she sobbed brokenly. "Oh, Mama," she sobbed. "Mama."

"There, there," her mother said, patting her on the back and holding her tightly. "There, there. It's all right, sweetheart. Everything's all right now. We love each other. That's all that matters."

"I do love you, Mama," Delta said, hiccuping through her tears.

"And I love you," her mother said, squeezing her daughter tightly and smiling through her tears. "And I'm so *proud* of you! I'm proud of your books, but most of all, I'm proud of *you*—of your spirit and sense of humor, and the way you fought for Kyle just now, taking on your own sister."

"Half sister."

Her mother shrugged. "A quibble. We're a family, Delta. Let's begin acting like one."

Delta took a deep breath and wiped away her tears. Today had been the worst and the best day of her life. "Know what I could go for right now?" she asked suddenly.

"Not a Carnaby Chocolate Cream, I hope!" her mother cried, looking distraught.

Delta broke up laughing. "No," she said, hugging her. "A good five-mile run. Out in the clean, fresh air, with the blue sky overhead and the sun beating down and the forsythia just bursting into bloom."

"My God," her mother said, awestruck. "That man has gone and worked a certifiable miracle." Then a slow smile spread across her beautiful face. "But then love is always a miracle," she said softly, folding her daughter into her arms.

Fourteen

Delta lifted her face so that the makeup man could dust it a final time with a huge brush. Then she smiled nervously and got up from the chair. The television studio was a revelation. Watching from home, she had always thought the set was a comfortable facsimile of a living room. She saw now that the walls were fake and that the furniture was pushed into the center of a huge soundstage cluttered with cameras, lights and coils of electrical cable. And while she stood there, dozens of men and women raced back and forth, shouting orders and checking pieces of equipment.

Everyone was frazzled except Bill Morton, who slept in his dressing room until the last possible moment, then rose, dressed and sauntered onto the set, looking immaculate and affable. His blond hair was always sleek except for the adorable cowlick that was his trademark, along with the pipe he held almost as a prop. He would chew the pipe thoughtfully on the stem as he listened to his guests, then puff on it as he read his notes about his next one.

Delta shifted nervously from one foot to the other and glanced apprehensively at Marcia Howard, who was pacing back and forth, smoking one cigarette after another, looking like a storm cloud. Nothing like a little encouragement, Delta thought, then turned away from her editor and uttered a despairing prayer.

"You're on next, Ms. Daniels," a production assistant said, smiling encouragingly. "You can go out on the set when we cut for a commercial. I'll give you the signal."

Delta nodded and smiled nervously, and the assistant smiled back. "You don't have to worry about a thing. Morton's a pro. Even if he hasn't read your book, he's great at faking it."

"Even if he—" Delta's eyes widened. Oh, that'd be just great! On national television with a host who hadn't even read her book!

"Relax," the assistant urged her. "You'll do fine."

Delta nodded, then jumped when the assistant told her to get on the set.

"Relax?" she whispered shakily. "You've got to be kidding!" She stumbled over cables as she made her way to a couch, blinded by lights and suddenly frozen by the sight of the audience.

Bill Morton was reading over a note card and holding a copy of her book. "Yours?" he asked shortly.

She nodded dumbly.

"You nervous?" he asked.

She smiled stiffly. "No more than a murderer on death row."

"Piece of cake," he said, then grinned. "Sorry. Bad choice of words for a diet guru." Delta shrugged and felt a little more relaxed. Bill Morton glanced through her book, then asked, "Are you ready to respond to the questions my assistant went over with you?"

Delta nodded quickly, then smoothed nervous hands over her skirt, checking to make sure her slip wasn't showing.

"You look great," Morton said, smiling. "Your diet must work."

She looked up apprehensively. Was he kidding, or did he mean it? That morning she'd weighed in at a sleek and trim 125, but she knew the camera could add ten pounds and make her look like a plump teddy bear.

"Ten seconds," someone shouted at the edge of the set.

"Ready?" Morton asked her.

She nodded stiffly, then crossed her fingers. "Yes."

"Welcome back," Morton said suddenly, shifting into the charming manner that she was used to from watching him on television. "Our next guest probably needs no introduction. If you've ever been on a diet, you've probably tried one of hers, maybe even the one that's the subject of the number one bestselling nonfiction book for the past month. She's Delta Daniels, author of *The Last Diet Book You'll Ever Need*." He shifted his gaze toward her and smiled engagingly. "Delta, welcome."

She smiled and nodded. "It's nice to be here."

"How's a person get started writing diet books, Delta? Are you a certified nutritionist?"

His question left her blank. It wasn't one of the ones she'd practiced over and over with his assistant earlier that day. She blinked once, then shifted uncomfortably in her chair. Oh, well, what the hell. Damn the torpedoes and full speed ahead. "Actually, I started out writing comedy," she said. "Then I realized it would be funnier if a fat person wrote diet books, so I switched careers."

"A fat person?" It was Morton's turn to look startled. "Delta, honey, you're anything but fat."

"Not right now," she admitted, "but I have been." She rolled her eyes and was flattered when the audience laughed. "Boy, have I been!" More laughter rippled pleasantly through the audience like gentle waves in the ocean.

"You're kidding," Morton said, sitting up. He began to chew on his pipe stem animatedly. "Tell us about it. Did you follow your own diet when you lost weight?"

"Which time?" she asked dryly, and was again rewarded by audience laughter.

"You mean you've been fat more than once? I mean, have you gained the weight back?" Morton asked, sitting up even straighter, as if he'd sensed that this completely unplanned conversation just might have some magic in it.

"Hasn't everyone? It's a human phenomenon, I'm afraid. Most of us haven't the willpower to lose weight and keep it off. Sooner or later it comes right back on." She glanced off the set apprehensively toward Marcia Howard, but Marcia was looking interested, as if she too sensed that things might be going well. Delta continued. "That's one reason why I've written so many diet books. When one diet does its job, it's time to go on to the next. Unfortunately, most of us never come to grips with the real reason we gain weight."

"The real reason?" Morton asked, furrowing his brow.

Delta almost laughed out loud. Why, he was as much of a fake as she was! She had a sudden insight that the whole world was made up of imposters. Everyone was probably pretending they were at ease and sure of themselves, while feeling sick inside with apprehension that everyone else would find out the truth about them.

That insight, delivered in a flash of a millisecond, helped her relax. Suddenly she knew she had to be as honest as she could be. She had the power of television at her disposal and was going to use it if she could. She sat back, crossed her shapely legs and smiled easily.

"Bill," she said familiarly, and was rewarded with a look of astonishment from the famous host, "I've been battling the bulge for almost twenty years, and most of the time I've spent hiding from myself what it's all been about."

"What *has* it all been about, Delta?" Bill Morton asked in that sickeningly serious voice.

"For me," she said, "it's been about anger and jealousy and lack of love. Who knows what it is for other people."

"Anger and jealousy and lack of love," Morton said thoughtfully, biting on his pipe stem. "What do you mean by that?"

"I mean that I'm probably like a lot of people." She turned her face to the camera with the red light lit and continued speaking earnestly to her audience. "Most of us probably have some fears we never face. We run from the truth the way children run from shadows. But when we stop to face our fears, that's usually what they turn out to be—shadows. For me, I ate to compensate for feeling unlovable. It wasn't until I began to realize that I *am* lovable and that I deserve love that I began to really conquer my need to eat. I suddenly found out that I didn't need food as a compensation any longer. Now I felt entitled to go out and fight for what I *really* wanted."

"So what exactly are you suggesting, Delta? Are you in fact saying that women might not *need* your diet book?"

It was a trick question, but it didn't bother her. She smiled easily. "Not at all. I think a sound nutritional program will always be necessary, and I *do* confer with respected professional medical doctors and nutritionists, as you'll see in the introductions to any of my books. But I *am* saying that until people look into themselves and discover the reasons why they're overeating, they won't really ever win the battle of the bulge. They may win skirmishes, but they'll probably start gaining weight back again almost immediately after losing it, simply because they're only treating symptoms rather than root causes.

"Another thing," she said without pause, interrupting Morton before he could even phrase his next question. "I've recently been turned on to exercise. Like many overweight people, I've never liked to exercise—I equated it with torture. But with the help of an extremely able personal trainer, I've found that exercise combined with proper nutrition—such as you'll find in my latest book—along with a careful examination of one's own life and needs, is the way to permanent weight loss."

"Delta Daniels, our time is up," Morton said, smiling widely. "We're so glad you could be with us today on *Mornings with Morton*. Will you come again?"

"Sure will," she said cheerfully. "I'll have a new diet book out next year at this time, which I hope will find a home on the bestseller list for months."

"And you'll still be thin and looking radiant?" Morton asked flirtatiously.

She grinned and winked at him. "Sure will, Bill."

The audience laughed, and the director cut to a commercial. Then Delta was herded off the set where Marcia Howard threw her arms around her. "You were great, honey," Marcia said in her deep voice. "Who'd ever have thought you could get the laughs you did and still manage to get a serious message across?"

"Marcia," Delta said dryly, "I used to write for television, you know."

"No matter, no *matter*," Marcia said irritably. "What's important is, he asked you *back*!" Marcia's face lit up. "And the way you slipped in the plug for your book, and even better, the mention of the *next* book." Marcia looked at Delta with the affection only a mother can show her dearest child. "Honey, you're a *pro*! We'll have a new contract for you. How about something written about the exercise angle next time? Maybe you and this personal trainer can get together and come up with something. Eh?" Marcia grinned and winked. "Eh, Delta, honey?" she asked, elbowing Delta in the ribs.

Delta smiled and tried to escape the elbow. "It's a possibility."

"Good. Have a proposal on my desk by Friday and I'll see what I can do about sweetening the next contract."

"No sweets, Marcia," Delta said wryly. "Bad for the figure."

Marcia chortled gleefully, then her smile was gone and she was glaring at her watch. "Damn," she said wrathfully,

"I've got a meeting at noon and I'm late already. See you, Delta. Get that proposal in, you hear? Talk to you."

Marcia was gone in a cloud of expensive perfume and cigarette smoke, leaving Delta shaking her head.

"Hey," Morton said, running past, "you did great. Come back, you hear?"

"I will," she said, suddenly feeling somewhat dizzy. She wandered around until she found her way out and escaped to the train station, where she caught an express to Boston. She sat on the train for the next few hours thinking about Kyle, wondering if he had watched her performance. She hadn't seen him since he'd moved out on Monday. Her mother and Sheila had stayed until early yesterday, and the time had been spent in catching up and finding out how wrong she'd been about both of them, as well as in harder and more determined exercise. She'd even put herself back on an eight-hundred-calorie diet, something she was sure Kyle would have disapproved of, but which she felt she needed.

But when the train pulled into Boston, Delta's stomach was tied up in knots. She was nervous and bombarded by old urges that told her to pig out on a chocolate milk shake, french fries and God knows what else. Instead, she lunched abstemiously on a salad with low-cal dressing and sipped ice water, then made her way to the bus station, where she climbed aboard and promptly fell to biting her nails.

She had to see Kyle, she couldn't live without seeing him much longer. They had their future to settle, but if Kyle hadn't really meant it when he'd said he loved her, then maybe she could interest him in writing a book with her. At least that way, she would be able to keep him in her life in some capacity.

Delta was so tired she didn't even bother to put her car in the garage. She dragged herself into the house and collapsed into the first chair she found. Kicking off her shoes, she slumped across the table and closed her eyes as she slid fast toward sleep and oblivion.

"Tired?"

Kyle's voice brought her abruptly awake. She sat up as if she'd been shot from a cannon, then turned to see him lounging in the doorway to the family room. He was wearing faded jeans and a T-shirt that molded his fabulous chest. She felt her stomach do a crazy flip-flop, and her heart began to pound.

"Kyle," she squeaked. "What are you doing here?"

He dangled the house key in front of her. "I never gave the key to your house back. I decided I wanted to be here when you got home. I put my car in the garage." He dropped the key onto the kitchen table and began to massage her shoulders. "Feel better?" he asked.

She went limp. "God, yes," she groaned, then sat up and twisted in her chair to look up at him. "Did you watch *Mornings with Morton*?" she asked excitedly. "Did you see me? How'd I look? Did I look fat? Was I a jerk? Did I do okay?"

"One question at a time!" he said, laughing. "Let's see now. Yes. Yes. Great. No. No. Yes."

"Ky-yle!" she wailed. "Come on, be serious."

"I am. I've always been serious about you."

She went very still, then shifted her gaze uneasily from his. "Really, Kyle, did I do all right?"

"You were wonderful, just like I knew you would be," he said softly. "And if you don't believe me, you can watch for yourself. I taped you."

"Oh, God," she said, slumping over and hiding her head. "I couldn't watch myself. I just *couldn't*! Ugh!" Then she sneaked him a look. "How did I look?"

He laughed. "I told you, you looked great."

"Well," she said slowly, "maybe I could watch just a *little....*"

"Come on," he said, taking her by the arm and leading her to the study. "I've got it all set to go."

She sat forward and stared at herself, groaning and laughing. Then she hid her eyes, and at last, turning to Kyle with a serious look on her face, she asked, "Well? Tell me straight now, how was I?"

"I've told you, honey. You were terrific."

"Why'd you call me honey?"

"Because..." He shook his head and grinned. "Oh, no, you don't. The last time we talked, you said you hadn't forgiven me for inviting Sheila and your mother. Maybe we should clear the air first. Would you like to throw something at me? A chair perhaps? Or a sofa?"

"They wouldn't be big enough," she said dryly. "Or hurt enough. You deserve to be lynched."

"This sounds serious."

"It is. You interfered, Kyle. You meddled. Only mothers are supposed to do things like that. Just where did you get off taking matters into your own hands the way you did?"

He sighed and slid lower on the couch, stretching his legs out in front of him and resting his chin on his chest. "It worked, didn't it?"

"But what if it hadn't?"

"What would you have lost?"

"You!" she cried.

"But you wouldn't have," he assured her. "I wasn't the least interested in Sheila."

"Why not?" Delta asked. "You're the first man who hasn't been."

"Because she's not you."

Delta looked at him sideways, trying to catch sight of any untruths that might be lurking in the vicinity. "What's so special about me?" she asked doubtfully.

He shrugged. "Damned if I know. If I knew why people fall in love with the people they fall in love with, I'd become a millionaire. Take Harry—"

"*Who* is Harry?"

"He works in the gym. He's got a body that won't quit. He could have any woman on earth, but he fell in love with a little roly-poly dumpling of a girl with a Cupid's-bow mouth and bright orange hair, with freckles all over her face and upturned nose. He can't say why he loves her, but he does. It's the same with me. All I know is, whenever I see you, Delta, I get goose bumps. I start to hyperventilate. I see stars. I get hard—''

She felt her face go red. "You *what*?"

He grinned at her. "You heard me."

She nodded. "Yes, but I don't believe you *said* it!"

He drew her into his arms, but she went unwillingly, pushing as hard against his chest as he pulled. He won. "Delta," he crooned against her hair, "why fight it? It's destiny. It's been ordained. I didn't get married until now because I hadn't met you. You opened the door that day and I was sunk, but so were you. I'm not letting you get away, Delta. You're mine now, and that's final."

She closed her eyes and sank against his muscled chest, hearing the tempo of his heart and knowing that it wasn't lying. "You really love me?" she asked softly.

"I really love you," he answered, kissing her on the forehead.

She sighed and nestled closer to him, her eyes still closed, her lips curved in a dreamy smile. "I love you, too," she whispered.

"Then I think we should get married."

She sat up then, taken by surprise. "Isn't this a little soon to be talking about marriage?"

"Why?" he asked. "I love you and you love me. Why wait? Marriage takes enough hard work. We may as well get started now."

She shook her head at him. "You amaze me, Kyle Frederick."

His eyes grew darker as they wandered down her figure. "Wait till I get you into bed," he said huskily, picking her up in his arms and striding determinedly toward the stairs. "Then I'll *really* amaze you."

She put her arms around his neck and smiled. "What have you got planned?"

"Champagne and satin sheets," he murmured against her lips, kicking open the door to her bedroom and depositing her on the turned-down bed.

She looked around in surprise. He hadn't been lying. There were white satin sheets on the bed, champagne sitting in a silver ice bucket and red roses on the bedside table. Slowly he began to unbutton her dress.

"I thought you might like to celebrate a little," he murmured, dropping kisses down her throat and onto her breasts.

Breathlessly she put her arms around him, feeling warm and dizzy and wonderfully happy. "What are we celebrating?" she whispered.

"Your successful appearance on *Mornings with Morton,* for one thing," he said, sliding her dress and bra off, then hooking a finger into her panties and panty hose and taking them off with one fluid movement. He dropped a kiss on her midriff, then sat up and poured champagne into two glasses. He handed her one, then turned and pulled a rose from the bouquet.

"Here," he said. "For you."

She took the rose, feeling bemused, and lifted it to her face, then gazed down at it, startled. Nestled in the rose was a diamond ring, the magnificent multifaceted stone gleaming and winking in the soft light. She drew in her breath and picked the ring from its bed in the flower. "Oh, Kyle," she breathed. "It's beautiful."

He took it from her and slid it onto her finger. "Now it's official," he murmured, leaning over to kiss her gently.

"But what if I'd said no?" she asked, her eyes suddenly gleaming impishly.

He settled her back against the satin pillows and began kissing her lazily. "Do you really think I'd accept no for an answer?"

She laughed softly, wrapping her arms around him. "Do you really think I'd be foolish enough to say no?"

"Ahh, Delta," he whispered ecstatically. "Everything's perfect."

"Not quite everything," she murmured, sitting up.

"No?" he asked, frowning.

"No," she breathed, smiling as she began to unbutton his shirt. "You've still got your clothes on." She pressed kisses on his hairy chest and began to unbuckle his belt. "But give me a minute, and everything will be just fine."

Laughing softly, Kyle gathered her into his strong arms. She went willingly, radiantly, laughing with joy, knowing she'd found everything she'd ever dreamed of and more—a deeper understanding of herself and her family, the ability to finally control her weight and the true and lasting love of a wonderful man. What more could a woman want?

"Oh!" she said, sitting up suddenly. "Guess what? Marcia gave me this *great* idea! She suggested you and I do a book together on exercise and weight control. Isn't that wonderful? What do you think? Want to start now?"

He groaned and sat back, folding his arms behind his head. "Is it always going to be like this?" he asked with a mixture of exasperation and affection. "Me wanting to make love and you coming up with ideas for books?"

Startled, she stared at him, then began to smile. "Golly," she said, running her fingers down his bare chest. "Whatever came over me? I guess I got my priorities messed up for a moment there." Her fingers drifted down his body until she came to a stop. "Gee," she said, widening her eyes innocently. "I guess maybe we should do something about this, huh?"

He groaned raggedly and dragged her into his arms. "Yes," he said, laughing hoarsely, "you temptress. You did that to me on purpose, didn't you?"

"Uh-huh," she murmured, laughing softly, "but if you try very hard, I think you can distract me."

"How about being distracted the rest of the night?" he whispered.

She sighed dreamily and lifted her face for his kiss. "All night and all day," she breathed.

He kept her to her promise.

*   *   *   *   *

Silhouette Intimate Moments

MORE THAN A MIRACLE
by Kathleen Eagle

This month, let award-winning author Kathleen Eagle sweep you away with a story that proves the truth of the old adage, "Love conquers all."

Elizabeth Donnelly loved her son so deeply that she was willing to sneak back to De Colores, an island paradise to the eye, but a horror to the soul. There, with the help of Sloan McQuade, she would find the child who had been stolen from her and carry him to safety. She would also find something else, something she never would have expected, because the man who could work miracles had one more up his sleeve: love.

Enjoy Elizabeth and Sloan's story this month in *More Than A Miracle*, Intimate Moments #242. And if you like this book, you might also enjoy *Candles in the Night* (Special Edition #437), the first of Kathleen Eagle's De Colores books.

For your copy, send $2.75 plus 75¢ postage and handling to:

In USA
901 Fuhrmann Blvd.
P.O. Box 1396
Buffalo, NY 14269-1396

In Canada
P.O. Box 609
Fort Erie, Ontario
L2A 5X3

Please specify book title with your order.

Silhouette Desire

COMING NEXT MONTH

#433 WITH ALL MY HEART—Annette Broadrick
As soon as he saw beautiful, reserved Emily Hartman, charismatic Jeremy Jones knew they were from two different worlds. Could he find a way to join their disparate lives?

#434 HUSBAND FOR HIRE—Raye Morgan
Workaholic Charity Ames needed a temporary husband—fast! After taking the job, Ross Carpenter's ulterior motives were soon forgotten. This husband-for-hire wanted to be permanent!

#435 CROSSFIRE—Naomi Horton
Eleven years ago Kailin Yarbro had told Brett Douglass she was pregnant. He'd known she was lying—but now she was back, and there was a child....

#436 SAVANNAH LEE—Noreen Brownlie
Savannah Lee had promised to tame Blake Elliot's cats to prove that her cat obedience school was legitimate. Blake hadn't counted on her feline expertise taming *his* tomcat tendencies.

#437 GOLDILOCKS AND THE BEHR—Lass Small
When Angus Behr discovered "Goldilocks" sleeping in his bed, he knew he wasn't going to be able to let Hillary Lambert go—this she-Behr was *just right*.

#438 USED-TO-BE LOVERS—Linda Lael Miller
The powerful chemistry that had united Tony Morelli and Sharon Harrison with heart-stopping passion had turned into an explosive situation. Could they find a loving solution?

AVAILABLE NOW:

TALES OF THE RISING MOON
A Desire trilogy by Joyce Thies

MOON OF THE RAVEN—June
Conlan Fox was part American Indian and as tough
as the Montana land he rode, but it took fragile yet
strong-willed Kerry Armstrong to make his dreams
come true.

REACH FOR THE MOON—August
It would take a heart of stone for Steven Armstrong
to evict the woman and children living on his land.
But when Steven met Samantha, eviction was the
last thing on his mind!

GYPSY MOON—October
Robert Armstrong met Serena when he returned to
his ancestral estate in Connecticut. Their fiery
temperaments clashed from the start, but despite
himself, Rob was falling under the Gypsy's spell.

Don't miss any of Joyce Thies's enchanting
TALES OF THE RISING MOON,
coming to you from Silhouette Desire.

SD 432